Stepbrother, Mine

Stepbrother, Mine

Opal Carew

ST. MARTIN'S GRIFFIN

NEW YORK

This is a work of fiction. All of the characters, organizations, and events portrayed in this novel are either products of the author's imagination or are used fictitiously.

STEPBROTHER, MINE. Copyright © 2015 by Opal Carew. All rights reserved. Printed in the United States of America. For information, address St. Martin's Press, 175 Fifth Avenue, New York, N.Y. 10010.

www.stmartins.com

Library of Congress Cataloging-in-Publication Data

Carew, Opal.
   Stepbrother, mine / Opal Carew.—First edition.
      pages ; cm
      ISBN 978-1-250-05285-8 (trade paperback)
      ISBN 978-1-4668-5471-0 (e-book)
   1. Women college students—Fiction. 2. Man-woman relationships—Fiction. I. Title.
   PR9199.4.C367S74 2015
   813'.6—dc23

                 2015034717

The chapters in this book were previously published as individual e-books.
Stepbrother, Mine: Part One. Copyright © 2015 by Opal Carew.
Stepbrother, Mine: Part Two. Copyright © 2015 by Opal Carew.
Stepbrother, Mine: Part Three. Copyright © 2015 by Opal Carew.

Our books may be purchased in bulk for promotional, educational, or business use. Please contact your local bookseller or Macmillan Corporate and Premium Sales Department at (800) 221-7945, extension 5442, or by e-mail at MacmillanSpecialMarkets@macmillan.com.

First Edition: November 2015

10 9 8 7 6 5 4 3 2 1

To my readers
with my deepest appreciation

Acknowledgments

Thanks to my awesome editor, Rose Hilliard, for your infinite patience and support.

Thanks to my wonderful agent, Emily Sylvan Kim, for always working things out.

Thanks to Mark, Matt, and Jason. Love you always!

Thanks to all my FB friends and followers, especially those who share my books with the world!

Special thanks to Jessica Alcaraz and Romazing Reader! (You know why! ☺)

Part One

Dana stared at the letter in her hand, all the blood rushing from her face. Her fingers began to tremble and the paper nearly slipped from her grip.

She sank down in the chair.

"Hey, what's up?" her roommate, Elli, asked, as she walked past and slumped on the couch across from her. "You're white as a ghost."

"I . . . uh . . ." Dana glanced up at the slim, tall blonde who shared the small, two-bedroom apartment with her. It was a bit dumpy, but it was only a ten-minute walk from the university. "It's from my mom."

"Oh? What does the bitch have to say?"

Dana cringed a bit at the way Elli referred to her mom, feeling disloyal to her family for not sticking up for her, but at this precise moment, she didn't really feel like defending her mother. And Elli was only going on the incidents she'd witnessed.

"She . . ." Dana sucked in a deep breath. "She says I'm cut off."

"Cut off? You mean, she won't be giving you any more money toward your education?"

Dana shook her head. "She thinks it's a waste of money and time for me to go for my master's. She thinks I should go out and get a real job, and learn to stand on my own two feet. She won't even co-sign on another student loan."

Which was wholly unfair. Every time Mom had driven away another man, Dana had been there to pick up the pieces. To get her off the bottle and back on her feet so she could cope with the world again. Dana always had to be the adult, while Mom would wallow in her misery.

Dana gazed at Elli, her chest compressed under the weight of her crushed dreams. "I don't know what to do," she murmured helplessly.

Elli pursed her lips. "I think I have an idea, but promise me you'll keep an open mind, because it's a little bit crazy."

Dana stepped off the elevator of the big office building. Elli had accompanied her on the bus, as much to make sure she actually went through with it as to provide moral support. Now Elli waited in the lobby while Dana went to meet the photographer.

She'd filled out the forms on-line, knowing she could back out if she wanted to. She couldn't believe she was about to do this—sell her virginity to a billionaire willing to pay top dollar. But it made sense from a practical standpoint. She'd secretly wanted to get rid of her virginity since starting college, because everyone she told about it treated her like a freak. Rather than shed it at some lame party with a drunk college boy, why not get the money she desperately needed and lose her virginity at the same time? She wouldn't think too hard about the implications.

She opened the glass door and walked into a lavish reception area. On the walls were photographs. All portraits.

"May I help you?" the receptionist behind a high wood-and-glass desk asked.

"I have an appointment at two p.m."

"Miss Reynolds?"

Dana nodded.

The receptionist smiled. "Just take a seat."

Instead of sitting, Dana walked to the wall and glanced at the photographs. They were exceptional. The first several were stunning portraits of young women. Dana walked along, admiring each one. Then she came to one of a man.

He wore a suit and watched her with confident eyes, sending goose bumps along her spine. Was this one of the men who might . . . ? She sucked in a breath, then gazed at the next photo, then the next. Every one of these men gave off an aura of incredible power and confidence.

Her heart fluttered in her chest. Oh, God, could she really do this?

The sight of all these handsome, intriguing men had her certain she wanted to try.

Why did these men do it? Surely with their looks, money, and confidence they could have any woman they wanted. But that was another part she didn't want to think about too much. They were willing to pay, and that's what she needed.

"Are you ready for us to take your portrait for the site?"

She stood up. "Ready as I'll ever be."

"Is there anything else, sir?"

Mason glanced up from his paper to see Sylvie curtsying in front of him. She would be leaving very soon, so this was one last opportunity for her to take care of his needs. And hers.

The short, black uniform with the white lace apron and trim showed off her assets quite nicely. The full skirt was so short there was bare thigh showing above the fishnet stockings, held up by black garters adorned with white satin bows. Her long slender legs looked even longer in the black patent stiletto heels she wore.

It was a totally impractical outfit for a maid. But for a sub, it was perfect.

She stood waiting for his answer. He set his paper aside, considering the question. He could order her to do anything he wanted and she would do it. That was any man's dream, but he'd just spent the entire weekend commanding and controlling and, right now, he just wanted it to be easy.

He leaned back in his chair. "Yes, Sylvie. I'd like to come one more time."

She bit her lip. "Yes, sir. Of course, sir. And may I ask . . . ?"

"Yes, Sylvie. You can come, too."

She curtsied again. "Thank you, sir."

She reached behind herself and unzipped her costume, then dropped it to the floor. She wore very brief panties and a demi-bra that lifted her breasts while fully exposing her nipples. He expected her to kneel in front of him and take his flaccid cock from his pants, warm it up with her mouth, then climb on his lap and ride him, but instead she flicked her nipples with her fingers until they were hard and pouting. His cock stirred. Then she tucked her fingers into her panties and he watched the fabric move as she stimulated herself.

Even though his cock rose, he found his mind was wandering. What would he have for dinner once Sylvie was gone? The cook was off until tomorrow but had left him several choices. He ran through the menu options until Sylvie's moans drew his attention, and he focused on her rosy cheeks, noting that she was getting close.

"Sylvie, do not come until I say so."

She moaned again. "But I'm so close, sir."

He clapped his hands and she instantly drew her hand from her panties.

"I'm sorry, sir." Then she turned and scurried away.

He knew she'd done it on purpose. She knew when she protested, it meant punishment. She returned with a wooden paddle and handed it to him. He patted his lap and she stretched over it, her sweet ass pushed upward over his thighs.

He raised his hand and smacked her cheeks with the paddle. She cried out. But he knew she wanted more. He struck her again. Her skin blushed red. He kept on paddling her—lightly at first, then harder.

He preferred to spank a woman's round behind with his bare hand, but Sylvie liked the paddle. Lily, on the other hand—one of his other subs—loved it when he smacked her bare bottom, then stroked his palm over it.

Sylvie's moans increased—he'd barely been aware of them until now. He rested the paddle on her bare, red ass and waited.

"Oh, please, sir. Don't stop."

He raised the paddle and began smacking in short, quick strokes. Her moans increased, becoming more intense.

"Oh. Sir. Please," she said between smacks. "May. I." She moaned again. "Come?"

"Yes, Sylvie." He kept paddling. "You may."

She arched against his hand. He stopped paddling and stroked between her intimate folds, as he knew she liked at this point. She was dripping wet and as he slid his fingers inside, her muscles gripped them tightly.

Soon her wails filled the sizeable room, echoing off the walls. His cock twitched with need.

He kept stimulating her, keeping her orgasm going on and on.

Finally, her moans subsided and she slumped on his lap. After a moment, she stood up and curtsied again.

"Thank you, sir."

Then she knelt in front of him. She unzipped him and within moments, her warm lips surrounded his cockhead. Fuck, she was the only one of his subs who could take his whole length down her throat without gagging. He closed his eyes as she bobbed up and down, keeping him warm and stimulated in her hot mouth.

His mind wandered back to when Lily had sucked him off last weekend. She had a tongue piercing, which added a little extra something. All his subs had their own idiosyncrasies. Lily loved to struggle against him, pretending he was taking her against her will. That still excited him. One of the few things that still did.

He typically had three or four regular subs at a time. He would spend the weekend with one, or sometimes two of them. They all knew about each other. When he got bored, he would bring someone new into the mix. It took time to train a sub, so he didn't have short-term relationships with women. In a Dom-sub relationship, it took time to get to know each other's wants and needs. It was an investment of time and energy.

The problem was, he was getting bored with his current subs. All of them. But he didn't have the interest to take on training a new sub.

Sylvie sucked hard and his cock lurched. He cupped her head and guided her forward and back. His body was demanding his attention as his cock throbbed inside her mouth.

Then Sylvie drew back, exposing his cock to the cool air. He groaned.

She smiled, clearly sensing she'd lost his attention and glad to have it back. She stripped off her panties and handed him the paddle again, then leaned over, offering her bare, red ass to him. He smacked her bottom a couple of times with the paddle and she moaned. Then she positioned herself over him. He groaned again when her hot opening pressed against him. She lowered herself onto him, her tight passage swallowing his cock inside its hot, velvety depths.

She leaned forward and kissed him, a light brush of lips, then she started moving on him. Driving his cock into her body again and again.

He gripped her hips, guiding her into a rhythm that felt good, his cock pulsing with need inside her hot core.

Heat swelled within him and he drove her body up and down faster as his engorged cock throbbed. She moaned in pleasure, and he realized she was coming again. He groaned and his cock erupted inside her.

He collapsed in the chair, spent. She leaned against him, then nuzzled his neck. He wrapped his arms around her and held her. She was sweet and sexy, and she'd just spent the entire weekend pleasuring him. As he had her.

But now he was just anxious for her to go.

He was bored.

Mason sat in the leather chair at the desk in his den and opened his browser. He reviewed his e-mail and added a few things to his calendar, then sighed and glanced at the clock. His dinner would be in the oven for another fifteen minutes.

A chat window popped up. It was a message from his friend Guy.

Hey, your SL gone home already?

Guy called Mason's subs "sluts"—in fact, he called the women he himself spent time with "sluts," too—but he knew Mason wouldn't put up with it, so he called them "SLs," which he said was short for "slave," but Mason knew he was just yanking his chain.

Yeah, Mason replied. He didn't feel very talkative.

So, all alone in your big house. Bored, yeah? You really should look into that service I was telling you about. FYI, they just got a new batch of SLs. Or should I say, SL-wannabes. ☺

Then a link appeared in the chat window.

Guy knew Mason had been bored lately and told him he needed to shake things up sexually. Then he'd told him about this service that allowed young women to essentially sell their virginity to wealthy men for a hefty sum of money. The fee was fifty grand. The guys who frequented the site could drop that amount without batting an eye and some justified it by saying it was doing a great service because most of these young women were college students who used the money to pay for their education. In fact, it had been dubbed "The Scholarship Fund" by the men who used it.

Guy had closed his chat session, but Mason found himself staring at the link.

He had absolutely no interest in deflowering some virgin, but he couldn't help wondering what kind of women would allow themselves to get involved in this kind of thing. Why did they resort to selling their bodies? Didn't they have parents who could help them? Were they too lazy or inept to earn the money on their own?

He found himself clicking on the link.

A black screen opened, displaying a simple insignia with a lone field underneath, requesting that he enter a code. Guy had told him that one had to be registered to enter the site. And Guy had paid the thousand dollars to register him as a birthday present last month.

Mason entered the username Guy had given him. *BoredDom.*

A new page displayed. He selected the page that talked about the types of women available through the service. It gave a pitch about how wholesome and *safe* they were, how enthusiastic the young women were to have this opportunity, and generally made the whole thing sound like a bunch of Girl Scouts wanting to sell cookies to help the poor.

He clicked on the link that would allow him to view the women currently available. He wondered if they would be naked or in seductive poses. When the page came up, it offered various selection criteria based on physical appearance, age, education level, et cetera. He just clicked on "New Arrivals."

A new page opened and he stared at a list with pictures on the left and brief bios on the right. The four photos visible on the page were all of quite lovely-looking young women gazing at him with bright smiles, wearing normal street clothes, sitting in chairs with their hands folded in their laps.

The photographer was excellent because he had somehow managed to capture a distinct personality in each of them. They were all posed the same way, and they all smiled, but the first one clearly had an impish side. Maybe it was the way her lips turned up that gave that impression, or the glint in her eyes. The second seemed more timid. The third, he sensed, would have a fiery temper, even though her hair was golden blonde rather than red.

He scrolled down the page, viewing each smiling face. The timer on his phone sounded, indicating that his dinner was ready. He glided his cursor up to close the window when his eye caught on one of the smiling faces.

He frowned, then stared at the familiar smile and wide, innocent eyes. But he must be mistaken. He clicked on the link labeled "Details" and a larger picture of the woman appeared. His stomach clenched. Fuck, it *was* her. He glanced at the name to confirm.

Fuck, what the hell was Dana doing on a site like this?

•   •   •

Dana stepped out of the lecture hall and followed the flow of students out the front door. Elli was waiting for her outside at one of the picnic tables on the grass. Dana sat down beside her. They were going to meet some of their friends, then head out for a coffee.

"So how'd you do on your psych paper?" Elli asked.

"Okay. I got an A-minus."

Elli laughed. "Most people would say that was great, not just okay." Elli wrapped her arm around Dana and hugged her close. "But that's okay. I love you despite the fact you're a brainiac."

Dana laughed. "Thanks. I love you despite the fact that you're a jerk," she said with a playful wink.

Dana's phone plinked and she pulled it from the pouch on her backpack. She glanced at the text.

"Trinity says she's going to be a bit late."

Elli laughed. "What else is new?"

Dana opened her e-mail to check her messages. There were a couple, but the sight of the last one caused her chest to constrict.

It was from the service. She opened it and her heart stalled.

"What's going on?" Elli asked. "You just went white as a ghost."

"I . . . uh . . ." She glanced up at Elli. "They got back to me."

"Who?" Then Elli's eyes widened. "Oh, you mean . . ." Then she grinned. "Hey, that's great. So you have a taker?"

Dana nodded, numbness creeping through her.

Then she sucked in a breath and started shaking her head.

"I can't do this." Dana stared at the e-mail, butterflies having a rave in her stomach. "I don't know what I was thinking."

"Are you kidding?" Elli said. "Fifty grand and you're set. That'll cover tuition and living expenses, right? What's your other option, Dana? Drop out and work a minimum wage job for the rest of your life?"

She glanced at Elli as if pulled out of a dream. "No, of course not. It's just that I need more than that, so this doesn't really solve my problem." She frowned. "And with a master's in French poetry, I might wind up working for minimum wage anyway."

Unless she managed to become a professor, though she knew that wouldn't be easy. But it was her dream and she'd decided long ago to follow her dreams with tenacity. After all, no one else was going to look after her happiness. It all depended on her.

"All the more reason for you to do it. It does solve a *big* part of your problem. Then maybe you can get a job for the rest."

Dana fiddled with the plastic cover on her latte. "I don't know. I'm not sure the visa allows that."

How could she sit here calmly talking about how she'd arrange her finances while staring at an e-mail offering her fifty thousand dollars for her to give up her virginity to a total stranger?

"You'll figure it out." Elli nudged her arm. "Now answer it before you change your mind."

"Are you not hearing me?" Dana said frantically. "I've already changed my mind."

"Dana."

At Elli's serious tone, Dana met her gaze.

"It's your decision, but I still think it's a good idea. I gave my virginity to a dumb jock in high school, and all I got out of it was a pregnancy scare."

She leaned forward, and Dana stared into Elli's calming brown eyes.

"All you have to do is sleep with some hot, sexy, *billionaire*."

"He might not be hot and sexy."

"But that's not what you're worried about. You're worried about the fact he's a stranger. Well, just think of it as a blind date. You'll meet, you'll see if he seems nice, and if you're attracted to him. And you don't have to worry about him hurting you or anything, because Sammy told me that these guys are cleared, and they're told if they do anything the woman doesn't like, they'll be held accountable. Including being banned from the service."

Elli squeezed Dana's arm. "This place is reputable and wants to stay in business. Everything is going to be okay."

Having made the decision, Dana felt a calmness come over her. A day after she'd answered the e-mail, she received confirmation, telling her she was to see a lawyer who would have her sign a contract. It was a fairly simple agreement that laid out the understanding. She would meet with the man and then decide if she wanted to go through with it. If she did want to proceed, there was another paper she would sign once she decided.

A date was selected for her to meet with him—two weekends from now—and a limousine would pick her up to take her to the meeting. Probably at a hotel—Elli told her that most of the men didn't want the women to know their real addresses so there'd be no chance of the women bothering them afterward. This was meant to be a one-time thing, though the one time might occur over a weekend or several dates, depending on what the particular client wanted and what made the woman comfortable.

Dana's particular "sponsor," as they called them, wanted her to come for the weekend. The lawyer explained that it would give them time to get to know each other.

After meeting with the lawyer, Dana went to an appointment with a personal shopper. The woman took her measurements and asked her many questions about her color and style preferences for clothing, even having Dana select various wardrobe items from pictures. She had half-expected lingerie, but the woman showed her everything from jeans and casual tops to evening gowns, shoes . . . everything. The personal shopper explained that it helped her to understand Dana's taste. Clearly, Dana's benefactor wanted her to be comfortable in what she wore on this sinful weekend, which was a good sign.

Finally, the day arrived. Usually she spent the better part of her weekend doing her assignments for the following week, but she'd worked frantically to ensure she had them all done.

She grabbed her overnight bag and walked down the stairs and out the door of her small apartment building. She was told she didn't need to bring anything, but she had her toiletries, her own pajamas, and a few books. And her laptop. Surely there'd be some time for her to spend by herself to catch up on her e-mail and maybe do some of next week's readings.

A black limousine pulled up in front of her and the driver got out of the car.

"Ms. Reynolds?"

"Yes, that's me." She shivered a little, wondering whether the man who was going to . . .

She sucked in a deep breath.

Was her sponsor in the car?

But when the driver opened the door for her, she saw it was empty inside.

She tried to relax as the car glided along the road. There were refreshments within easy reach, but she ignored the individual-size bottles of wine, beer, and soda. Instead she grabbed a water bottle and opened it.

So this was it. She'd made the decision and was now in a big, fancy limousine on her way to meet the man who would bed her and take her to womanhood. She shivered at the realization that her deflowering would simply be a business arrangement. Meaning nothing to the man except a diversion. Whereas to her it would be . . .

What would it be, exactly? When she was younger, she'd thought it would be a momentous occasion. Something a woman never forgot.

As she got older and her friends started losing their V-cards, though, she realized it wasn't such a big deal. But then why did she feel like she was about to lose something important? She rested back in the seat.

She could get all depressed thinking about giving it up to a stranger, to whom it meant nothing.

Or, she could think of it as her defining moment. A moment where she decided to take advantage of what she had to offer and leverage it to give herself the future she wanted.

But that was all too distant. The man was going to kiss her. Touch her. Make her feel things she'd never felt before.

For that one time, she was going to be the center of his attention.

She closed her eyes. What did he look like? She imagined a big, broad-shouldered man in a suit sitting beside her, leaning in close. He cupped her face and lifted it toward him, his deep blue eyes locking on hers. And his face . . . oh, God, it was *his* face.

She had dreamed of him for years. And in those

dreams, she was able to explore what she could never contemplate in real life.

His lips took hers and she melted against him. Loving his powerful hold on her as he drew her close to his body. Her heart beating frantically as his lips moved on hers, and his tongue pushed between her lips and claimed her mouth.

Oh, God, she'd always dreamed that he would be the one to take her to womanhood, but that would be unthinkable. It just couldn't be.

He had walked out of her life forever, so even if it hadn't been forbidden, it was clear he didn't want anything to do with her anyway.

She was tired of being abandoned by others. She was in charge of her own life now. Not like when she'd been younger. When her mother and others had still had the power to make her feel helpless and alone.

Ten Years Earlier

Dana was sixteen years old and her mother had done it again. Gotten married. But not like a normal divorced mother who would introduce her intended to her daughter to let her get used to the idea, then have a wedding, and then move her daughter and herself into their new home.

No, *her* mother met the guy on vacation, married him in some exotic location, then proceeded on an around-the-world cruise with him, sending her daughter a letter apologizing for the delay in returning. Then she had her lawyers arrange to have the house sold, and to have Dana and her stuff picked up and dumped on the steps of her new stepfather's house.

An impressive home, she realized as she stared at the huge entryway and the tall columns rising up from the marble floor. Mom had money from her previous divorces, and so Dana was used to living in nice homes, but this place . . . this mansion . . . was huge and the height of elegance.

But also cold. And cavernous.

The butler took her bags and led her to her room. Or rather, "her quarters," as he called them. She stood in the doorway, stunned at the opulence of the place. It wasn't just a bedroom. It had a living room and a dining room attached. And even a small kitchen stocked with snacks.

"Dinner will be served at eight," the butler informed her. "Please don't be late." Then he turned and strode away.

Once she'd settled in, she left her quarters and strolled around, wanting to familiarize herself with the place. It was so big and daunting. There were a few servants around, but they just ignored her.

She managed to find the dining room and was surprised to find only one place set. She shouldn't really be surprised. She knew Mom was still away, but a small part of her had hoped that her mother had actually returned to surprise her. That she wouldn't really just leave her here all alone in this new, strange place.

But, no. That night Dana ate alone, then returned to her room and cried herself to sleep. The next morning, she ate breakfast alone, and the butler guided her to the front door, where a limo waited to take her to school.

A week went by with her going to school and returning to the big, lonely house. She might as well have been living there all alone. She cried herself to sleep most nights, wishing she had someone to talk to. Her friends at school didn't understand. She was living in a huge house, with a pool and tennis courts. What more could she possibly want?

It was Friday night and she wondered, if she asked for the chauffeur to drive her to the movies with her friends, would he do it? She tried to get the nerve up to ask, but finally decided the stress wasn't worth it.

As she opened her book bag and pulled out the weekend's homework, a knock sounded at her door. She dropped the books on her desk and walked toward the door.

The butler never knocked, leaving her to her own devices. Had someone come to visit her?

She pulled open the door, then stared in awe at the handsome man standing in the doorway.

Present Day
"We're here, Miss."

The driver stopped the car and got out, then opened her door and helped her from the car. They stood in front of a tall, elegant-looking building. It didn't look like a hotel. More like a luxury apartment building. The driver rolled her overnight bag to the front door and the doorman opened the door for her. The driver led her across the impressive lobby—with its marble floors, tall pillars, and huge floral arrangements—to an elevator.

"This is a private elevator." He slid a card into a slot and the door opened. "It will take you to the penthouse." Then he handed her the card and walked away.

The door closed and her stomach fluttered as the elevator started moving upward.

When the door opened, she stepped into a huge apartment with windows overlooking the city. She stepped from the elevator onto the gleaming, dark hardwood floor of the foyer, expecting her benefactor to be waiting for her. But there was no one in sight.

She glanced around at the elegantly furnished penthouse, with light walls and leather couches and chairs. The wood furniture had clean lines and large pieces of abstract art hung on the walls. The whole look was balanced by the softness of the plush carpets and cushions.

She walked across the floor and stared out at the city below. The sun was setting and the windows of the other buildings were bathed in orange light.

"Like the view?" a male voice asked from behind her.

A prickle started along the back of her neck, then moved down her spine.

It wasn't the voice of a stranger.

It was *him*.

She turned slowly, her heart pounding in her chest.

"Mason?" Astounded, she stared at the man she hadn't seen in eight years.

"Hello, Dana."

The shock of seeing him had thrown her totally off balance, but now she remembered the situation.

"Oh my God, you're the one? But . . . you can't . . . ," she sputtered.

He raised his eyebrow in that way she remembered. "Can't what? Be the one who takes your virginity?"

Her eyes widened. "That's right. We just . . . I mean . . ."

She stared at him—the man who had left when she was eighteen. The man who'd made her feel special and cared for in a time when she had felt like nothing.

The man who haunted her hottest and most forbidden dreams.

She sucked in a breath and tried again. "You're my stepbrother, for God's sake."

The second Mason laid eyes on her, his breath caught. Dana had been stunning even at sixteen, but now . . . Good God, she just oozed alluring-yet-innocent sexuality.

"*Ex*-stepbrother. Which doesn't really count."

He had lived in the same house with her when his father had been married to her mother, but only briefly, so it didn't really count as a familial relationship, but that didn't change the fact that he had no intention of taking her to bed.

His intent was to shake her up, and ensure that she didn't try a stunt like this again. Because whether they were actually related or not, he had an intensely strong protective instinct where she was concerned. He always had.

He stepped toward her and she stepped back, then started to walk away. He grasped her arm and pulled her toward him, determined to push her to the limit.

"We haven't seen each other in a long time. Don't I deserve a kiss?"

He pulled her against him and into his arms. He had intended it to be just a quick brush of lips, wanting to shake her a little, but the feel of her softness against him threw him off-balance.

She sucked in a soft breath just before his lips captured hers, then the sweetness of her mouth became a temptation he couldn't resist.

His tongue swept between her lips and she whimpered softly. A vibrating need pulsed through him, his groin tightening with a desire he would not allow.

He drew back, blanking his expression as he stared down at her wide eyes. As soon as he released her, she skittered across the carpet to the couch, putting it between the two of them.

"You can't really mean it. You don't really intend to . . ." She frowned, her cheeks a vivid red.

He walked to the big armchair and sat down, then gestured for her to sit on the couch facing him. Warily, she walked around the couch and sat down.

"So tell me, Dana. Why are you selling your body?"

"I'm not selling my body. I'm . . ." She wrapped her arms around herself, hugging tightly.

He raised an eyebrow. "Really? What do you call it?"

"Okay, yeah. That's exactly what I'm doing. But just this one time."

"This *first* time."

Once he'd gotten over the shock of seeing Dana on a website offering to sell her virginity, he had wondered how she could claim she was a virgin, since he had assumed she had given that up on her prom night. But he'd never doubted her honesty.

"Look, it's not a big deal. It's just a business arrangement. People have sex all the time." She shrugged. "It's like a blind date, that's all. With someone who's been recommended by a friend."

"Really?"

"Well, yeah, in that I know the guy will be safe. The service is really careful."

He thought she was being more than a little naïve.

"You still haven't told me why you're doing it."

"I need the money for school. It's enough to pay for my tuition until I graduate. It's really important to me and this is the only way I can afford it."

He already knew this, but he wanted her to face what she was doing. To justify it out loud so she could realize what a bad idea it was.

"Why? Won't your mother pay for it?"

Dana shook her head. "No."

"Why didn't you work hard? Get a scholarship?"

Fire blazed in her eyes. "I did."

"So what's the problem?"

She hesitated. "My grades dropped last year." But she said nothing more.

He crossed his arms. "I'd ask if it was because of a boy, but since you're here it means you clearly weren't screwing around."

She pursed her lips. "It was my dad. He got very sick last year." Her eyes glistened with moisture and he wished he hadn't pushed her.

"Dana, I'm sorry. I didn't know. Is he all right?"

She shook her head and dashed away a tear. "He died. Six months ago."

Ah, fuck. He stood up and walked to her, then settled down beside her. "I'm sorry. I know you were close."

He drew her into his arms and held her. She rested her head against his chest as he stroked her hair back.

She'd always been a smart kid. Good in school. Bringing in the best grades in the class. But the distraction of her father being sick, then losing him. Of course she'd lost her scholarship.

He held her for a few minutes, comforting her. But her softness against him soon gave his body a different idea.

Fuck, if this weren't Dana, he'd be pulling her into his

arms and ravaging that sweet mouth of hers until she was breathless.

Dana's heart pounded in her chest. Being held by Mason like this was so comforting. He was the only man, besides her father, she'd ever felt safe with.

He had been twenty-six when she and her mom had come to live with him and his father. Dana had been sixteen, and she'd idolized him. Like his father, he was handsome and confident. And he'd taken an interest in her, trying to get to know her. Wanting to make their little family work.

But she'd developed a huge crush on him. He might have been her stepbrother, but to her he was a handsome, sensitive guy who paid her a lot of attention and actually seemed to care about her. More than any of her stepfathers had.

More than her mom ever had.

He'd always had a lot going on, working at his father's business, and following up ideas of his own, but when he was home, she'd hang out with him as much as she could. She remembered one time when he'd gone away to a conference for a week, and when he'd come home, she'd flung herself into his arms and hugged him, never wanting to let him go.

Then she'd kissed him.

That kiss had surprised them both. It had deepened to one of passion, her heart pumping faster and harder than it ever had. A deep yearning had started inside her and she knew now, looking back, that if he'd been a different man—one willing to take advantage of a young woman—that he could have taken her on the spot.

But he wasn't that kind of man.

At least he hadn't been. But now . . .

She drew away from him.

He'd bought her virginity. Pure and simple. And he'd already shown his intent when he'd pulled her into his arms and kissed her.

She was shaken by that kiss. There had been nothing brotherly about it.

This yearning for him had been with her since she'd first met him ten years ago. It still blazed inside of her.

In truth, if she could choose any man in the entire world to be her first, it would be him.

But now, in this situation . . .

Oh, God, could she go through with this?

She gazed up at him. "So what now?"

Was he going to lead her into his bedroom and . . . carry on? The thought both excited and terrified her.

He sighed as he stared at her with his serious blue eyes.

"Dana, I didn't bring you here to follow through on the agreement."

She blinked at him in surprise. "What do you mean?"

"I mean I'm going to give you the money you need for your education. No strings. Nothing required of you."

"Why?"

"Because I care about you. Because I want to help."

She shook her head. "But you can't just give it to me."

"Of course I can."

She stood up and paced. This couldn't be happening. She wanted the money. Desperately. But she refused to take handouts.

"If you're having trouble with the idea of me giving you the money, I could make it a loan."

She bit her lip.

Oh, God, it was a lot of money. When she'd thought she'd be earning it, it had meant she could go to Paris without a huge loan weighing on her, but if he loaned her the money . . . Sure, she would pay it back, but . . . who was she kidding? She had no idea what kind of job she could get with a degree in poetry. And that was a lot of money.

She wanted him to give it to her. But she couldn't accept it. Anger sluiced through her. If he had stayed out of it, then another man would have bought her contract and she wouldn't be faced with this dilemma. In fact, she'd probably be stretched out on the guy's bed right now, already finished.

A cold depression wafted over her.

Damn. She was so confused. She glanced at him and he just watched her as she paced.

Her stomach tightened and she stopped moving. "I can't. I just . . ." Her mind was a whirl of tumultuous thoughts and bewildering feelings. She rested her hands on the sides of her head, feeling like it was about to explode. "I need to think."

But she felt mired in the heavy weight of her thoughts.

"Dana, just relax. Sit here beside me and we'll talk it through."

He patted the cushion beside him and her head shook back and forth of its own accord. His familiar words didn't comfort her. So often he'd said them and helped her work through her problems. But she couldn't be that close to him. Not after that devastating kiss.

She backed away. "No, I can't . . ." Her gaze darted around the room. "Not here. Not with you."

She bolted for the door.

When Dana got home, she avoided Elli's persistent questions, closing her door and hiding out in her room. Then she tossed and turned all night.

Seeing Mason had stirred up so many things inside her, not the least of which was a massive longing to succumb to her desire for him. Although she'd been shocked at the idea of having him take her virginity after he'd bought the right through a service, she had always dreamed of him taking her in his arms and kissing her passionately, then proceeding to do exactly that.

But that was in her dreams, not in reality.

What he had said was true, though. They weren't really related. That meant that there was no real reason that they couldn't become intimate. Except for social convention, but that concern had gone out the window when she'd decided to sell her virginity online.

She rolled over and stared at the window. Moonlight streamed in and washed the room in soft light.

The fact that he'd wanted to protect her, and to help her by giving her money for her education, made her feel cared for. She couldn't accept it, but that didn't make it any less appealing that he wanted to help her.

She was so confused. He'd always been so good to her, and so good for her. He'd looked out for her and had seemed to really care about her.

Then one day, he'd simply walked out of her life. And at a time when the situation was pretty bad between their parents. She'd never felt so alone. Or so abandoned. And that was saying a lot.

Her heart ached. She'd always wondered if she had done something to drive him away.

She had been pretty needy, consuming as much of his time as he would allow, and along the way, she'd done a couple of things that were maybe a bit . . . off, from his point of view. Like that time she'd kissed him. And the things he hadn't known about. At least, she hoped he hadn't.

And then there'd been prom night. Her cheeks flushed at that memory.

Her hand ran over her jeans, resting over where the tattoo was. Oh, God, she could never let him see that.

But now he was back in her life and seemed to truly want to help her.

She had no idea what to do.

Ten Years Earlier

Dana blinked at the stunning figure standing in the doorway. He was the type of man made for a designer suit.

She was only sixteen, but she could tell that the expert cut of his tailored jacket accentuated every plane of his broad-shouldered, trim-waisted torso. The fine wool looked touchably soft yet crisp, giving the garment a professional, elegant look. She wanted to run her hand along his lapel, and not just to feel the fabric. Her insides quivered at the thought of touching this perfect, sexy man.

His chestnut hair was cropped short, but not so short as to do away with its soft waves. And his eyes. God, his blue-green eyes—almost teal, in fact—were breathtaking. A clear color that reminded her of the ocean, with darker rings around the pupils, giving them definition.

His jaw, square and masculine, was shaded with coarse whiskers that made her want to stroke it to feel the raspy texture.

"Are you . . . um . . ." She felt intimidated by the closeness of his big body, his teal eyes studying her. "Are you my stepfather?"

He seemed too young, even for her mother, but he did bear a striking resemblance to the portrait hanging in the dining room.

He laughed—a deep, rumbling sound that she instantly liked.

"No, I'm his son. Mason." He offered his hand. "Which makes me your stepbrother."

She placed her hand in his. His big fingers closed around her small hand and her breath caught at the heat washing through her.

God, her stepbrother. She thought she'd faint.

He shook her hand, then released it. He leaned against the doorjamb, peering into her room.

"So you're settled in."

She nodded.

"Kind of stuffy décor for a teenager. If you like, I'll see if we can get it redecorated for you."

"Oh, I wouldn't want to be any trouble."

He grinned and her heart skipped a beat. "Dana, you live here now. This is your home. Your room should reflect you."

She just nodded, not wanting to argue with anything he said.

She wanted him to come in. She wanted him to . . . Oh, God, she didn't know what she wanted him to do, but some deep, unnamable need filled her with yearning.

"I have an idea," he said. "It's Friday night and I'd love to just kick back and relax. How about pizza and a movie?"

"You mean, you and me?" she asked, wide-eyed.

"Yeah, sure. Why not?" He glanced down at his attire. "Don't worry, I'll change. I wouldn't want to embarrass you."

She shook her head. "Oh, no. You couldn't." She was stuttering like a child and her cheeks burned, but he chose not to notice.

In the end, they decided to order pizza in. When he returned in his jeans and soft, cotton button-up shirt, he looked every bit as devastating as he had in the suit. Instead of eating in the stuffy dining room, he invited her to his quarters—right next to hers—and they ate from the box, with cans of soda from his bar fridge. He asked her all kinds of things about herself—what she was studying at school, her favorite bands, her interests, and what her dreams and aspirations were. If this was what it was like to have a brother, she wished she'd had one sooner. More so, though, she wished he were her boyfriend. He was older—he had to be twenty-six or seven—but she longed for him to take her in his arms and kiss her.

But she quelled those disturbing longings. At least, she did her best to.

After the pizza, they watched an action movie together. But it had been a long week and, despite the explosions and fast-paced car chases, she dozed off. When she awoke, instead of finding herself leaning against Mason's big, solid body, she was stretched out on the sofa, and he was sitting in the armchair next to the couch, still watching the movie.

"Oh," she said sleepily, as she pushed herself back to a sitting position. "I . . . uh . . . didn't mean to . . . um . . . hog the sofa."

"Don't worry about it. You were tired. I thought you'd be more comfortable with the couch all to yourself."

She flushed as she realized she'd probably snuggled against him and it had made him uncomfortable. How embarrassing. He must see her as some silly little teenager and could probably tell that she was crushing on him like crazy.

Yet he was so nice about it. Not making her feel stupid. Putting up with her immaturity.

"I guess I should go to bed." She stood up and headed out of his quarters, then practically ran to hers and closed the door behind her. Once she was in bed, images of his big, masculine body and his handsome, smiling face haunted her dreams, making her want things she knew she shouldn't want.

As much as Dana was embarrassed by what had happened, she couldn't stay away from Mason. They ate breakfast together every morning and he dropped her at school on his way to work. The limo driver picked her up after, but Mason joined her for dinner every night. Even when he had to stay late at the office, he called and had the cook delay dinner so he could eat with Dana.

At night, when she lay alone in her room, she felt so lonely she could die. Mason made a point of spending time with her in the evenings when he could, but sometimes he had to work late. He told her she could interrupt him any time she wanted or needed someone to talk to—he worked in the office in his quarters in the evenings—but she didn't like to disturb him just because she was feeling lonely.

Even at the young age of twenty-six, he ran his own company. Apparently his mother had recognized his business acumen and given him money to start his own business when he'd been just eighteen.

Dana did go out with her friends sometimes, but when she'd done that pre-Mason, there'd been no clear time when she had to be home. The driver seemed to be on call twenty-four/seven, so she'd sometimes roll in at three in the morning. Not because she liked to be out that late—she'd always suffer at school the next day—but just because she wanted to see if she could. When no one seemed to care, she found it . . . disturbing. If she stayed out all night, she wondered whether anyone would even notice. And if something happened to her, would anyone know?

Now that Mason was here, he set a curfew for her. Not an unreasonable one, and he'd listen to her arguments for extending it. If she made a good case, he'd grant it. Her mother always seemed so inconsistent about whether she'd let her stay out or not. Sometimes a curfew was imposed and it was sacrosanct, never to be questioned. Other times, like recently, she didn't even notice that Dana was gone. Mason was so much easier to deal with and she felt that the rules he made were for her own good, not just to exercise authority like her mother did.

One night, a few weeks after she'd moved in, she awoke from a bad dream. She couldn't remember the exact details of the dream, but the shadows on the walls from the bushes swaying in the wind outside, and the small creaking sounds—probably the house settling as her mother always said—had her clinging to the covers and pulling them close to her face.

She lay there, trying to go back to sleep, but terror

rose in her. Finally, she pushed back the covers and tip-toed from her room. She knew the combination to Mason's quarters—he'd told her in case there was an emergency in the middle of the night—so she tapped it into the lock. She pushed open the door and tiptoed into the living area. His quarters, like hers, were open-concept, with the living room, dining room, office, kitchen, and bedroom all open and visible to each other (though the kitchen did have a counter with bar stools that blocked any dirty dishes that might be in the sink. Although Mason kept the place spotless, not leaving it to the servants to clean up after him.)

She gazed across the large quarters and saw Mason asleep in his bed. She didn't know why she'd come here or what she intended to do now. She would love to climb into bed with him and snuggle against his big, solid body. If she woke him up and explained that she'd had a bad dream, he would probably take her in his arms and hold her, comforting her. Maybe even brush his lips against her forehead. Maybe that would lead to a real kiss, and then . . .

Oh, God, that wouldn't happen. It could never happen. Not because she would stop him. No way. But because she knew in her heart that he wouldn't let it.

So if she woke him, he would comfort her. She was sure of that. But then he'd send her back to her own room to sleep.

And she didn't want that. She wanted to be near him.

So she grabbed the soft, cashmere throw draped over

the back of his couch, lay down, and covered herself with it. The couch faced away from the bed, so he wouldn't see her if he woke up, but she could hear the soft sound of his breathing and that was comforting. She knew he woke up at seven-thirty, so she set the alarm on her phone for seven, on vibrate. Then she let the sound of his breathing lull her to sleep.

In the morning, she awoke from the vibrating of her phone and sneaked back to her room. When she and Mason met for breakfast, he seemed to be none the wiser. Since it worked the first night, she decided to do it again the next night. And the next. Soon, it became an addiction.

Weeks went by and she and Mason grew closer. The days went by in a wild haze of happiness. Mason came home every night and spent time with her, making her feel important and . . . well, loved. He was like a real older brother, someone who genuinely cared about her.

What she longed for was for him to be her boyfriend. For them to go out on dates and hold hands. For him to cuddle her and . . . kiss her. Her heart stuttered at the very thought.

But he was her stepbrother and he looked out for her. That was enough for now.

And all of her friends were blown away by how totally dreamy her stepbrother was. It was especially cool when, one night, he picked her up in his black Jag instead of the limo. All the girls watched her climb into the sporty

car with the exceptionally handsome man wearing designer aviator sunglasses, and nearly swooned. She simply
smiled and enjoyed the wind in her hair as they drove
along the highway with the top down.

Life couldn't be better.

Mason pulled into the huge garage beside their mansion and parked his Jag, then opened her door. She followed him past the vintage cars to the entryway to the
house and inside.

"Good evening, sir. Will you be dining this evening?"
the butler asked.

"No, James. Dana and I will be having Chinese."

"We will?" Dana asked, hot on his heels.

She followed him up the stairs to his suite and then
inside. He pulled a bag from his jacket pocket and waved
it in front of her.

"You remember that video game you've been waiting
for?"

Her eyes widened, but she knew it couldn't be the
game inside. "Yeah, it comes out in two weeks, three days,
and five hours."

"Well, I happen to have some connections and I was
able to score an early copy."

"No way!" She snatched the bag from his hand and
peered inside. "Oh, my God. You did!"

She laughed and raced to her room to change, not
letting go of the disc package, then she raced back in her
jeans and cotton sweater. She popped the disc into the game

unit as he finished ordering Chinese food. They played until the food arrived, and then they played after they'd finished eating.

Finally, at eleven o'clock, he leaned back. "Okay, it's eleven. We both have to get some sleep."

She grinned. "I can do with only a few hours."

He laughed. "Yeah, well, I'm older and more decrepit. I need my eight hours, so out."

She pouted. "But *you* have the game unit." Then she grinned. "I could put on my headphones, so you wouldn't hear a thing, and keep playing."

"Okay, you. Out," he said, pointing to the door.

She pushed herself to her feet and walked to the unit, then ejected the disc. He raised an eyebrow.

"You don't think I'm leaving it here so you can practice without me, do you?"

He laughed. "Good night, Dana."

She placed the disc carefully in its case and closed it, then gazed at him. He was so good to her.

She ran to him and threw her arms around him. "Thank you so much for getting the game for me."

He did so many thoughtful things for her and, well, she loved having someone who actually cared about her and what she wanted.

"I've never had anyone . . ." She squeezed him tighter and his arms came around her to return the hug. "No one's really cared about me like you do. I mean, except my dad, but I hardly ever see him."

He patted her back and she ached at the comforting feeling he gave her.

And more. His body was strong and masculine and the feel of it against her triggered a deep yearning inside of her.

Finally, he loosened his arms around her. "Dana, you really need to go."

His voice was low and . . . she could almost believe she was affecting him . . . in that way. But he released her and stepped back and she knew it was just wishful thinking on her part.

"Thanks again," she said timidly.

He smiled, setting his handsome face aglow. "You're welcome. Now go."

She left his suite, the game clutched tightly in her hand, and headed back to her room, where she changed into her pajamas. She waited for about an hour and then sneaked back into his room. Closing the door quietly, she tiptoed to the couch and settled onto it, her phone alarm set as usual.

At one point, she woke up to a change in his breathing. She peered over the back of the couch, but he was still asleep. He'd simply rolled over. She settled back to sleep.

She awoke again several hours later and realized it was almost seven. Her phone would be vibrating to wake her up in about ten minutes. She peered over the back of the couch as she did every morning. The room was filled with the faint rays of early morning sun, and the sight in front of her took her breath away. Barely twenty feet away, Mason was lying on his stomach . . . and the covers were fully tossed back.

And he slept naked.

She drew in a deep breath at the sight of his naked butt. She stood up and walked toward him, assured he was still sound asleep by the sound of his deep breathing.

Oh, man, he had the tightest, sexiest ass she'd ever seen. Her face flushed as she realized she should *not* be seeing her stepbrother like this.

But her gaze lingered on his broad shoulders, then down his muscular back to his compact butt. Across one cheek the word "Courage" was written in script.

Then his breathing sputtered and he rolled over. Her heart leapt but she could not pull herself away. Now he was sprawled on his back, his tight, sculpted six-pack exposed . . . and a huge erection pointing straight up.

She sucked in a breath. She had never seen a penis before. Ever. And certainly not one at full mast.

Oh, God, it was huge.

Her phone vibrated in her pocket and she pulled it out.

She stared at him, her heart pounding. Then—not knowing why she did it—she flipped open her phone and snapped a picture of him in all his naked glory.

Present Day

Dana remembered how she used to sneak into Mason's suite at night. No hanky-panky. He wasn't even aware she was doing it. She'd just sleep on his couch for the comfort of being close. To hear his steady, even breathing and feel safe knowing he was nearby.

Though she'd always wished that she could climb into bed with him and snuggle close in his arms. At that age, it'd been almost as innocent as that. Almost. But as she'd gotten older, and other feelings had awakened, she'd desperately wanted to be in his arms for other reasons.

The morning she'd woken up to see him stretched out on his bed, the covers kicked back, his totally naked body exposed . . . Oh, God, she'd had some interesting feelings that morning.

If he had woken up and found her staring at him . . . He would have been shocked and definitely would have sent her away. She was sure he'd never felt that way about her.

At least, not when she was sixteen.

By the time she was eighteen, she'd started to think she'd sometimes see a glint of interest in his eyes. But he would never have acted on it.

Except on prom night, she'd almost believed . . .

God, no, she would not go there. She had to think about what was going on right now.

He had actually bought her virginity. Whether he took it or not was another matter, and he certainly seemed disinclined, but . . . She realized she still wanted that more than anything. She had never stopped dreaming about being with him, even after he had disappeared from her life without even a good-bye.

The fact that he'd shown up in her life again, wanting

to help her, meant that he hadn't stopped caring about her after all.

And the fact that he did still care about her made her want him all the more. And why couldn't she have what she truly wanted, at least this once? He wanted to help her, and she was a grown woman, after all.

And he was a man.

She sighed. What if things had gone differently and he hadn't told her he'd just let her off the hook? If he had actually intended to act on the contract, she'd be in his arms right now. The deed done and the two of them holding each other.

Maybe even doing it again.

Her insides melted as she thought about his big arms around her. His hands stroking her. Cupping her breasts. Oh, God, her hand stroking over his swelling cock. The feel of the hot hard flesh in her grip.

She still had that picture she'd snapped and, God help her, she still looked at it. A lot.

She grabbed her laptop and dug through her files until she found it. And opened it. Her insides heated at the sight of him lying on his bed, his huge cock standing tall and proud.

Oh, God, she'd had this fantasy often, but now with the very real possibility that it could come true, heat sizzled through her.

Her insides melted as she thought about that big, hard cock brushing against her intimate flesh, then his thick shaft pushing into her. Slowly, until he filled her completely. Then him gliding back and filling her again. His thrusts slow at first, then getting faster and faster.

Her fingers found her wet folds and she stroked as she thought of Mason's body above hers as he thrust into her, moaning her name. Driving her pleasure higher and higher.

She sucked in air, then moaned as her fingers flicked over her clit faster and faster, finally shooting her over the edge.

She awoke in the morning, still damp and sweaty from her nighttime fantasies. She showered and took a walk in the fresh air, wondering what she should do next.

Mason nursed the drink in his hand, still thinking about his encounter with Dana earlier this evening.

Well, that hadn't gone very well.

Damn, he shouldn't have tried to scare her off what she was trying to do. Though, what else could he do? He couldn't abide the thought of her selling her virginity to some rich playboy who just saw her as a plaything to deflower. Just because the guy was rich didn't mean he'd treat her well.

Mason wanted Dana to give herself to someone she loved. He was actually rather proud of her for having saved herself this long, but now that she saw her virginity as a commodity, she would probably try again.

Even if he somehow convinced her to take his money for her education, she still might try a stunt like this in the future.

Thoughts of Chas crossed his mind, and he shuddered. It would be just like the old man to check out a site like this. Thoughts of that lecherous asshole seeing Dana's picture there, buying her contract, and then . . . fuck, he could not let that happen.

Ten Years Earlier

Mason started from sleep with the feeling that someone was watching him. He opened his eyes and glanced around, but couldn't see anyone. Fuck, when he realized the covers were tossed off his body, he pulled them back on.

He knew that Dana often came into his room after he'd fallen asleep. One time when he'd been restless and woken in the middle of the night, he'd noticed her sleeping on his couch under the coverlet. He'd considered waking her and sending her back to her suite, but he knew the poor kid felt lonely in the big, strange house. She was just looking for comfort.

Thank God she hadn't tried climbing into bed with him because he might have had trouble controlling himself. She was so sweet and innocent, but also sexy as sin.

He'd realized she was probably coming into his suite regularly and had decided to leave it be. But waking up now with no covers hiding his naked form was a wakeup call. From now on he would don pajamas at night.

Mason got up, showered, and dressed. He knew that his father was returning today, so he decided to stay at the house rather than go into the office. His father was intimidating at the best of times. He didn't want to leave Dana to deal with him without support, and he doubted her mother would be much help.

Mason spent the morning working at the desk in his suite, and then after lunch, he and Dana read in the main living room, which had a big window facing the front yard.

Mason sipped his drink, glancing out the window as a sleek black limo pulled up in front of the house. The servants, who had been on alert for the past hour awaiting his father, scurried to the car to retrieve luggage. When the driver opened the door, a woman took the driver's hand from inside the limo and smiled as she stood, then looked at the large house with satisfaction. She was slender and well dressed in a designer suit, with a huge diamond flashing on her finger. Dad never did skimp when it came to diamond rings for his wives. Or any other jewelry, for that matter. It was his way of displaying his wealth. Have an appropriate wife, with the appropriate wardrobe to show off at the country club and social affairs. He never loved any of them. And he always had at least one mistress at his beck and call.

Dana sat nervously beside Mason, watching along with him.

"There's Mom," she said, fidgeting. "Are you sure I should wait in here?"

"Yes. Let them get inside and settled."

Watching Dana's mother outside, he could tell she was

the type of woman who liked to make an entrance, and having the servants scurrying around her made her beam like a queen. He was pretty sure she would resent her daughter for taking away any of her thunder. And he was pretty sure Dana knew that, too, because if she and her mother had been close, he doubted the woman would have abandoned her daughter here the way she had.

Dana watched intently as Mason's father—her new stepfather—stepped from the car and walked toward her mother. He smiled at his new wife's look of awe at her new home. He took her hand and kissed it, then guided her forward.

Dana took Mason's hand, her fingers trembling.

"It's okay. He won't bite," Mason murmured to her. Mason would make sure of that.

The big doors opened and his father and new stepmother swept into the house. When his father's gaze fell on Mason, his smile faded.

"Mason. What are you doing here?"

"I live here, Father."

His father's eyes narrowed but he said nothing.

"Who is this handsome young man?" Dana's mother asked. The bitch hadn't even glanced at her daughter yet.

"This is my son, Mason," was all Dad said.

Mason could feel Dana by his side, practically vibrating with the need to be noticed.

He shook the hand his new stepmother offered him, then glanced pointedly at Dana.

Her mother's gaze finally fell to her, then she pursed her lips. "Oh, Chas, this is my daughter. Dana."

"Oh, yes. Nice to meet you." His father's gaze barely flickered over her face, then fell to her outfit. "I hope you dress better than that when you leave the house."

Mason could feel Dana tense beside him. She had spent hours trying to pick out something nice. He had told her to wear what she usually wore. She had a particularly nice turquoise knit pullover sweater that set off her eyes that Mason loved seeing her in. But she'd wanted to impress his father and she'd picked out a pretty little dress that was demure though stylish and quite suited her. But his father just trashed it.

Dana glanced to her mother, but the woman's focus was sweeping across the opulent entryway, clearly wanting to see the spoils of her new allegiance, showing no concern at all for her daughter's discomfort.

"I'm famished. James," his father said to the butler. "Arrange a meal. Twenty minutes in the dining room." He glanced at his wife and new stepdaughter to ensure they'd heard him, then dismissed them. "Mason, in the den." Then he walked across the room.

Mason followed him down the hallway to the large den off the back of the house, and closed the double French doors behind them. His father sat at the big desk, as he always did when he wanted to intimidate, but it no longer worked on Mason.

"So you're living here now?" he asked with raised eyebrows.

"It's just as much my house as it is yours." Mason's mother had ensured that in the will. In fact, Mason owned it outright, but he'd promised his mother he'd let Chas continue to live there for a few years. More to keep up the pretense of them having been a happy family. The wealth his father enjoyed had come from his mother's family and she knew her husband wasn't good with money, so she'd wanted to ensure her family home stayed with Mason. But he was a bigger man than to point that out.

Chas frowned but nodded. "So at twenty-six you're okay living with your parents."

Mason perched on the mahogany credenza and smiled. "That all you got, Dad?" He shook his head. "Because being here doesn't threaten my masculinity one bit."

His father's face turned sour. He hated that Mason didn't cower in his presence.

But long gone were the days when Mason was intimidated by his asshole of a father. Not since Mom had given Mason a separate fund to start his own company when he was eighteen and he'd built his own fortune.

"So did you fuck the little tramp?" his father asked pointedly, his stare piercing through Mason.

He knew Chas was referring to Dana and it turned his stomach that his father would even hint at such a thing.

He scowled "No, of course not."

"Good. Make sure you keep your hands off her."

Mason stood up, his face solemn. "And I recommend you do the same."

His father's angry glare didn't fool Mason at all. There

had been rumors about other stepchildren. Mason couldn't prove it, but the rumors were enough to keep him wary. He was not naïve, and he had a strong feeling that Chas hadn't picked this particular woman *despite* her having a teenage daughter, but *because* of it.

Dana was a lovely young thing, and his father was bound to have seen pictures of her. He tended to have his future spouses checked out thoroughly by a P.I. before he proposed. He probably had all kinds of photos of Dana as well as of her mother.

That's why when Mason had heard that the old man had married again, and it was a woman with a sixteen-year-old daughter, he'd decided to move back in.

He couldn't believe that the mother had allowed the girl to be moved in on her own while she and her new husband were off traveling for months, leaving her alone in the huge mansion with no one looking out for her. When they came back, if his father did indulge in some vile activities with the young girl, her mother seemed like the type who'd take her husband's word for it over her daughter's.

Mason intended to stay here and make sure that didn't happen.

Present Day—A few days later
Mason glanced up from the couch as the elevator doors opened onto his penthouse.

Only someone with his key card could use the elevator. That meant it must be one of his subs. There was no one else he had given the card to.

To his surprise, Dana stepped out and gazed across the room.

Ah, he had given a card to Dana and she hadn't returned it when she'd run off.

He stood up as she walked forward. "Dana, it's nice to see you."

"Thank you. I'm sorry to just come in. I . . . still have the key card." She held it out to him but he just shook his head.

"Keep it," he said simply.

She bit her lip and slipped it into her jeans pocket.

"To what do I owe the pleasure of your visit?"

She walked across the carpet toward him. He gestured for her to sit down so she sat beside him on the couch.

"Have you come to accept my offer?"

She frowned. "Um, yes and no."

He tilted his head. "Really? And what does that mean, exactly?"

He could see her small, delicate hand trembling and he wrapped his fingers around it.

"It means . . ."

He squeezed her hand and smiled encouragingly.

"It means that I want to accept the money, but I can't just take it."

"So you want it as a loan?"

She shook her head. "I want you to do what the contract says."

She tightened her fingers around his hand and drew it closer to her.

He frowned. "What are you saying, Dana?"

Her cheeks flushed. "I'm saying I want you to be the one who takes my virginity."

There, she'd said it.

Now she stared at him, biting her lower lip, her stomach contracting.

What did he think? That she was a slut? Was he shocked?

His enigmatic blue eyes gave away nothing as he sat considering her.

"Dana, you don't have to tie the money to that contract. You aren't bound by—"

"No, it's not that. I . . ." She blinked, searching deep inside herself for the courage to say what she needed to say. She sighed. "I've always had a crush on you. You must know that. Then when you left . . ." She frowned, not really wanting to bring that up, but what else could she do? "I missed you so much. I never got over it. If it really was just a teenage crush, wouldn't it have faded by now?"

"Dana, I—"

"No, please. Let me finish. I know you probably don't feel the same way, but we're both adults now and . . . well,

I'd much rather lose my virginity to you than to anyone else in the world."

"Dana, you should keep that gift for someone you care very deeply for."

"But that's you. You've been one of the most important people in the world to me." She took his hand in both of hers and squeezed. "I know you'll treat me well and . . ." She bit her lip. "It would be so special."

He ran his hand through his hair.

"Is it that you don't want to be with me?" she asked, feeling very vulnerable.

"Fuck, Dana. You're a beautiful woman."

"But you still think of me as a teenager." She pressed her hand to his chest, feeling his heart beating. "But I'm a woman now. With needs." She smiled tremulously. "And I want you to meet them." She stroked his cheek. "I . . . I know I can trust you."

Then she leaned in and kissed him. He sat stiffly at first, then his lips lost their rigidity and he returned the kiss. His arms came around her and pulled her tight to his body as his lips moved on hers. Emboldened, she traced her tongue over his lips, then glided inside. He moaned and his tongue thrust into her mouth and plundered it as she felt herself pressed back onto the couch, him above her.

She sucked in air as his big body covered hers, his hands gliding over her back, his tongue filling her mouth.

When his hand glided down her side, lightly brushing

her breast, she gasped, then pulled her mouth free, staring up at him with wide eyes.

The simmering heat in his eyes startled her. She'd always hoped he returned her feelings of attraction, but this blatant confirmation was unsettling. She wanted this— so much—but it unnerved her all the same.

He drew her back to a sitting position.

"Dana, are you absolutely sure this is what you want?"

She just nodded, unsure of her voice right now.

"Well, I'm not sure about this."

She clutched at his lapels. "Please don't turn me down, Mason."

His lips compressed. "I'll need to think about it. In the meantime, I'd like us to get to know each other again. Spend some time together."

"Anything you want." She would do anything to make this happen.

The following Friday, Mason picked Dana up at her apartment in his limo. Three hours later, the car pulled up in front of the mansion where she had lived for two years. And where she'd met, and lived with, Mason.

The driver gathered their luggage and Mason opened the front door, then gestured her inside. She stepped into the entryway and glanced around.

"It's just like I remember it."

"Nothing's changed. Chas moved out about five years ago. I come here a couple of times a year, but mostly it sits empty."

"That's a shame," she said, gazing at the big staircase with the oak banister, spiraling upward to the private rooms upstairs.

She had loved this house when Mason had been in it, but once he'd left, she'd found it cold and lonely. She wished she knew why he'd left, but she didn't know if she'd ever find the courage to ask him. More because she was afraid she had been the reason, and she really didn't want to know that.

Especially not now when her dream of being with him, at least for a short time, just might become a reality. She didn't want old memories to ruin what was happening right now.

"So, want to race to our old rooms?" he asked with a grin.

"Oh, I wouldn't want to make you feel old when I beat you."

"Ha," he said, then lurched toward the stairs.

Watching him in his designer suit, running up the staircase, made her laugh, but not before she raced after him. The butler—someone new—watched them without even blinking.

Mason beat her to the door of her room. He laughed, then punched in the combination. The door opened and she peered inside. It was exactly as she remembered it.

They'd never redecorated. It had felt old and stuffy when she was sixteen, but now it felt elegant and luxurious with its cream velvet couch and chairs, rose satin drapes, and four-poster bed, dresser, and bedside tables in ornate cream-stained wood. The dining area and office nook were in the same style of wood furniture, all with soft, rounded shapes.

The artwork on the walls was very feminine. Mostly flowers and some paintings by Tricia Romance. One had become her favorite: of a young mother holding her curly-haired toddler in her arms, ribbons flowing from their hair. Sweet love emanated from the painting, and Dana had always wished she'd had a mother who adored her like the woman in the painting clearly did her own daughter.

The butler appeared with her luggage and brought it in the open door.

"You get settled in," Mason said. "Then come to my suite when you're done. I have a surprise for you." He smiled. "And if you're going to change, do you have anything turquoise? I still remember how lovely you looked in that turquoise sweater you used to wear."

She started. In fact, she knew exactly which sweater he was referring to. She had been wearing it the first time she'd met him, and he had told her several times how much he liked it on her. So she could never bear to part with it. She'd even brought it.

"I do. In fact, I brought that same sweater for old times' sake."

He beamed. "Well, since you did, I'd love you to wear it."

Then he slipped out the door and wandered down the hall, following the butler with his own luggage.

A surprise? Maybe he'd bought her some sexy lingerie. That would mean that maybe tonight would be their first time together.

Her stomach fluttered. She hoped their first time wouldn't be their last time, too. But he'd invited her here for two weeks, so she had high hopes.

She unpacked her bags into the drawers of her dresser— except the turquoise sweater, which she placed on top— then hung up her dresses. She placed her book bag on the desk, then she pulled off her shirt and put on the sweater. It was a little snug over her breasts, which made it look sexy. She went into her bathroom and ran a brush through her long, dark hair until it gleamed.

About fifteen minutes later, she walked down the hall and stared at the door to Mason's suite. Finally, she knocked.

A moment later, he opened the door.

"There you are." He smiled and gestured her in.

She couldn't help but notice the way his gaze dropped to her sweater and lingered, then his deep blue eyes heated.

Butterflies fluttered through her stomach as she stepped into his suite. Her gaze fell to the couch where she'd spent so many nights cocooned in the comfort of the soft, cashmere throw, with Mason's even breathing nearby.

"Sit. Are you hungry?" Mason sat on that same couch, patting the spot beside him.

Oh, God, he was so handsome in his snug jeans and blue striped, casual shirt.

"What's the surprise?" She glanced around, hoping to see a box wrapped with a big ribbon. She'd open it and pull out a skimpy, lacy, next-to-nothing negligee.

"Well, I have the same movies that we watched the first night we met. And pizza will be here in about five minutes."

"From Genario's?" she asked. If the surprise wasn't going to be a skimpy bit of lingerie, then a pizza from Genario's, the best she'd ever eaten, would be the next best thing.

Mason grabbed a couple of sodas from his fridge and placed one in front of her. The same type she'd had that first night.

A knock sounded at the door, then the butler opened it at Mason's invitation and carried in a large pizza box that he placed on the coffee table. The aroma emanating from it was heavenly.

"Would you like me to serve it, sir?"

"No, Henry, we can manage."

"Very good, sir." Then Henry disappeared out the door.

Mason opened the box and served her a big, gooey piece of pizza, placing it on one of the two fine, bone china plates he had stacked on the table. She took a bite, enjoying the dreamy delight of the rich, cheesy slice.

She sat back on the couch. "It's been so many years. I was only sixteen that first time we met."

"Sweet sixteen."

She frowned. If he kept thinking of her as that young teenager, he'd never do what they'd come here to do. She leaned closer. "But I'm not sixteen anymore. I'm a grown woman."

He laughed. "Down, girl. We're going to spend some time together to get reacquainted, remember? You are not dragging me off to bed before I'm ready."

She pursed her lips. "Shouldn't that be my line?"

He grinned. "By all means. Tell me to keep my hands to myself and give you space."

She smiled. "But I'm not going to do that. You can invade my space all you want."

His expression turned serious as his gaze locked on her. She shivered as he leaned closer, heat blazing from his intense blue eyes, and she found herself leaning away.

"Do you want me to take you now?" he murmured, his voice deep and seductive. His hand brushed her arm, sending sparks flashing across her nerve endings. "Right here on the couch?"

She could see the need in his eyes. The blatant desire.

She found it hard to catch her breath. "Uh . . . well . . ."

The intensity of his deep blue eyes, simmering with heat, unnerved her. She wanted this. Wanted to feel his hands all over her. But right at this moment, she wasn't feeling quite as ready as she'd thought.

Then his lips curled up in a smile. "Or do you want to relax and watch the movie?"

She nodded. "The movie."

He was right. She wasn't ready. Damn. He was always looking out for her. And he always seemed to know what she needed better than she did.

They finished the pizza and he turned down the lights as they settled in to watch the second movie, but she soon started to get sleepy. It had been a busy day at school, then the three-hour drive here. Soon she dozed off.

Then she started awake and realized the closing credits of the movie were scrolling on the screen. She glanced around and realized she was leaning against Mason's strong, sturdy body, his big arm around her. Just like the first evening they'd spent together, she'd fallen asleep, but last time she'd found herself lying on the couch alone, with Mason in another chair. He'd given her space. This time, he hadn't moved away.

She snuggled closer, wishing he would sweep her into his arms and carry her to his bed.

He flicked off the TV.

"Hey, sleepyhead. Time for bed."

She smiled up at him. "Okay."

He chuckled. "I didn't mean mine." He stood up and took her hands, then drew her to her feet.

"So you really want me to go back to my room?" she asked.

"That's the plan."

She sighed and headed for the door.

"And I assume you'll be back after you change to sleep on my couch, as always."

She turned to face him, eyes wide. "You knew?"

He grinned. "Not at first, but yeah, after a while I figured it out."

"And you didn't stop me?"

He shrugged. "I knew you were lonely. And as long as you stayed on the couch, I didn't think there was any harm."

She smiled as she trotted to her room. Once she'd changed, she headed back to his suite. She'd take his couch over her lonely bed any day of the week.

Mason heard the door open and Dana come into the room. The lights were off, but moonlight streamed in the window so he could see her small form move to the couch and settle onto it.

He'd been used to her sleeping there when she was younger, but even then, it had caused him some restlessness. Now, knowing what they were going to do, or at least, what she wanted him to do, was causing him more difficulties. In the form of a straining hard-on.

Fuck, he would love to drag her into his bed right now and sink his painfully hard erection into her soft body, but he wasn't really comfortable with this whole arrangement. He was hoping they would get to know each other anew and she'd become comfortable with him again. Even reconsider the whole thing and decide to take his money as a gift.

That's what he'd hoped, but the way she looked at him made him seriously question his plan.

As did his raging erection.

And he couldn't even find relief. Not with her sleeping less than twenty feet away.

Fuck!

He finally fell asleep, but it was a restless night, and he woke up with a raging erection again. He grabbed his robe and headed to the bathroom, where he took care of things in the shower. When he came out, he found that Dana had already left. Just like when she was younger, she'd probably set her phone alarm to wake her before his normal rising time.

That day, they drove into town and looked around, and later played some tennis. Then they went in the pool. Seeing her in a skimpy bikini wasn't the best way to keep himself sane in this situation, but she had a beautiful body and he couldn't help but admire it.

Dana loved how Mason couldn't seem to keep his eyes off her while they lounged by the pool. He certainly did seem to find her attractive and she loved the feeling. And watching him, his muscular body tight and sculpted all over, was like heaven. Especially as he dove into the pool.

That evening, she was hopeful that things would progress to the bedroom, but any time she even hinted at moving forward, he teased her out of it. By the third night, she was determined to make something happen.

She decided to try something crazy, so she went into town to shop on her own, telling him she had some lady things to buy. Then after dinner, she slipped back to her room and changed.

Mason rested on his couch and sipped his beer. He didn't know what Dana was in the mood for tonight. She'd said something about a game, so he suspected she'd return with a favorite video game.

A knock sounded at his door, then it opened.

When he saw what Dana was wearing, his mouth gaped open.

She was dressed like a sexy maid. Fuck, the neckline of the buttoned top dipped low enough to reveal a huge amount of cleavage. More than he ever suspected she had to reveal. And the short, flouncy skirt revealed her long legs, made all the longer by the six-inch spiked heels that she wore. The skirt didn't hide the sexy garters she wore, nor the strip of bare thigh above the black stockings.

He just stared at her as she walked toward him. His cock swelled, pushing uncomfortably against his jeans. God, he wanted to fling her onto the bed and run his hands all over her.

But why the hell had she chosen a maid costume, of all things? The sight of it brought up bad associations. Maria had done a number on him. He didn't mind fucking his subs in maid costumes. In fact, it was a real turn-on. Probably helped him to exorcise, or at least replace, his memories of Maria. But he wouldn't do that with Dana. He couldn't.

"I thought we might try a role-playing game," Dana said as she sashayed toward him.

But his anxiety turned to anger and he snapped at her, "Take off that costume."

Her eyes widened.

"Now, damn it!"

Before he knew it, she had stripped off the top and dropped it on the floor, her eyes wide.

"No, Dana, I meant—"

But before he could finish, she'd tugged off the skirt and dropped it, too.

Had she reacted to his command without thinking? Heat rushed through him at the thought that she might be a natural sub. *His* natural sub. Where she just automatically responded to his commands.

Fuck. She stood there in a black lace push-up bra that showcased her beautiful breasts. She still had the white, frilly apron around her waist, hiding her panties from view.

His heart raced and, as much as he wanted to order her to cover up . . . he couldn't.

"I didn't mean for you to take it off here," he muttered once he found his voice.

"I'm sorry, but you yelled at me and I just . . . did it." Her voice sounded shaky.

"I didn't yell."

She pursed her lips. "True. I just . . ." She raised her wide-eyed gaze to him. "It sounded like an order."

"It was, but . . ." Fuck it. He wasn't going to explain

his intent. Right now, she was standing in front of him, practically naked, and he was having a hard time remembering why he wasn't pulling her into his bed and driving his hard, aching cock into her.

"Never mind."

He stood up and walked toward her. Her cheeks flushed a pretty pink as he approached. He stopped in front of her and stared down at her soft, creamy breasts.

"You really want me to take you, don't you?"

She gazed up at him, her eyes glittering, and nodded. But he could see it in her eyes. The nervousness.

He took her hand and led her to his bed, then sat down and drew her between his knees.

"You have beautiful breasts, Dana. Do you mind if I touch them?"

"No," she said, breathlessly.

The sound of it made his cock lurch to attention. Her breasts were at his eye level and he reached out and stroked one fingertip across the top swell of them. God, they were so soft and silky.

She reached behind her.

"No, Dana." But he was too late.

She unfastened the bra and rested her hands on the cups, then her gaze locked on his, her cheeks flushing even darker, and she pulled it away.

"Fuck." The sight of her pert breasts—their tight little nipples peaking straight at him—took his breath away.

"God, Dana. They're perfect."

"You said . . ." She drew in a deep breath. "That you wanted to touch them."

He smiled. She certainly was eager.

He reached for those perfect mounds and cupped them. They filled his hands, the tight little buds pressing into his palms. He closed his fingers around them and kneaded them.

She made a small, strangled sound in her throat.

"Do you like that?" He wasn't sure if the sound indicated pleasure or something else.

"Oh, yes."

He chuckled, then glided his hand under her breast, lifting its weight, and stroked her hard nipple with his thumb. Her eyelids fell closed and her head tipped back.

"So beautiful, baby." He leaned forward and ran his tongue over the puckered nipple, then drew it into his warm mouth. Aroused by her small moan, he began to suckle.

Her fingers slid through his hair and she pulled him tight to her bosom.

He sucked harder.

"Oh, yes," she cried.

He smiled and moved to the other breast, then suckled until she was moaning steadily, her head tossed back.

He chuckled. "You're going to get a sore neck like that."

He stood up and wrapped his hands around her waist and set her on the bed, then he knelt beside it. He lapped at her nipples, moving from one to the other until her head was flinging back and forth on the pillow and her moans filled the room.

Fuck, she was so responsive to his touch. His cock ached to be inside her, but he would not allow that.

She was clearly turned on and he was dying to know how much. He began to lift her apron, wanting to get at the silky panties underneath, but suddenly she sucked in a breath and pressed her hand down on the apron, stopping him from lifting it.

"What's wrong, Dana? Do you want me to stop?"

"God, no. But I . . . uh . . ."

He waited patiently.

"I just don't want you to . . . uh . . . look."

His eyebrow arched. "Really?"

"I thought you would . . . I mean, if you go inside . . . you don't have to look, do you?"

"Well, I prefer to. I mean . . ." He stroked his hand over the apron, close to—but not touching—her mound. Wanting to tease her. "But, baby, I'm not taking anything from you today."

She frowned. "You're not?"

He smiled. "No. But that doesn't mean I'm not going to *give* you something."

He slid his hand under her apron and glided along the silky skin of her hip, until he reached her panties. He glided over them and flattened his hand on the crotch. Her eyes widened as she gazed at him, then he pressed his fingertips into the fabric and felt the dampness there. "Oh, baby, you are definitely ready."

She nodded. "I've been trying to tell you that."

"Yeah, you coming in here in a sexy maid costume did give me the idea. But I mean that, right now, you are physically ready." He stroked over the panties, pressing his fingers against her intimate flesh. "Are you sure you don't want me to see?" he asked, coaxing. Wanting to see her sweet little pussy so bad.

But she nodded. "But please don't stop touching me like that."

He laughed. "Here, this will be even better." He slid his fingers under the panties and groaned as he felt her soft, wet flesh against his fingertips.

"Oh, yes," she said breathlessly. "That is better."

She reached down and tugged on the apron, pulling it up a little at a time, until it revealed the crotch of her panties, but no more.

He didn't know what she was hiding, but as he watched his fingers moving under her panties, and she pulled the crotch of the panties to one side, he was glad it wasn't her perfect little pussy.

"Oh, baby."

Her folds were soft and pink, glistening in the lamplight. And totally shaven bare.

As he leaned toward her to get a closer look, she flattened her hand on her hip, holding the apron secure. He rested his hand over hers and patted, to let her know he would respect her boundary, then ran his fingertips over her exposed folds. He opened them with his thumbs, exposing her tiny bud, then he stroked it lightly.

She rewarded him with a soft moan.

He leaned closer and ran the tip of his tongue over it. She sucked in a breath.

He laughed joyfully, then covered her with his entire mouth. Her hot, moist flesh filled his mouth and he licked, tasting her sweetness. He buried his tongue inside her, pressing into her sweet, untried opening.

He lapped and swirled his tongue in her passage, loving her tiny murmurs of pleasure. Then he glided to her clit and teased it. Her sounds intensified and her hands clutched his head, her fingers raking through his hair.

"Oh, Mason. That feels so good."

The satisfaction of hearing her ardor-filled voice uttering his name with such need was indescribable. It filled him with such yearning that he could barely contain himself. His cock ached to escape and find her soft, moist opening.

He drove his tongue against her flesh, flicking and prodding. Driving her pleasure higher. She moaned and he could tell she was close. He began to suckle, gently at first, then harder. Her dampness filled his mouth and he sucked, drawing deeper on her little button.

"God, yessss!" She flung her head back and forth. "Oh, I'm going to . . ." Her hands tightened on his head. "Mason, you're making me . . . I'm coming!!!"

Then she moaned, loud and long.

His cock nearly burst on the spot.

He kept suckling, keeping her orgasm going and going.

Finally, she gasped and flopped back on the bed, panting.

He drew back and smiled at her. Then his heart clenched, totally unprepared for the absolute beauty of her face, beaming with euphoric afterglow.

He stretched out beside her, still smiling. He couldn't seem to stop.

She rolled against him and wrapped her arm around his waist.

"Thank you, Mason. I've never felt anything like that before."

"So I'm the first man to give you an orgasm?"

She drew back and gazed at him. "Well, yes. Of course. I thought you knew—"

"I knew you'd never had intercourse with a man, but that doesn't mean you've never fooled around a bit."

She shook her head. "No, never."

"So you've never touched a man's cock, either?"

She shook her head.

Suddenly, heat thrummed through him. He was the first to give her the gift of ecstasy. And . . . fuck . . . the thought that she'd never touched a man before made him want her even more. To possess her. To be the one and only whom she'd ever touched, or been touched by.

"You've never seen a man?"

He regretted the words as soon as they came out.

She dropped her gaze from his.

He knew she had seen a man before. And he knew she wouldn't lie about it, even though she didn't know he knew.

Fuck, he'd ruined the moment. Desperate to get it

back, he cupped her cheek and pressed his lips to hers. Her mouth opened and his tongue slipped inside. He explored her soft mouth, stroking with his tongue.

Then he felt her hand glide over his hip, to find the bulge twitching in his pants. He slammed his hand down on hers and slid it away, before he succumbed to the growing need inside him.

"No, we are not doing that."

"But, Mason . . ." Her big, blue eyes pleaded with him.

"I am not going to take your virginity tonight." If he had his way, he would never take it. "Be happy with where we are, okay, Dana?"

She pursed her lips, but then nodded.

"Okay." She rolled away and stood up, then walked toward the couch.

Her curvy, round ass was not covered by her apron, nor her skimpy panties, and his cock swelled at the sight of it sashaying away from him.

She gathered up the costume she'd shed on his carpet earlier. And the bra.

"May I borrow a robe?" she asked.

"Yeah, of course. In my closet."

She opened his bedroom closet and grabbed his plush robe, then pulled it on. She walked to the door of the suite, then turned and smiled sweetly.

"Thank you." Then she left.

He flopped back on the bed, his cock aching. He stood up and shed his clothes, turned off the light, and climbed into bed. Then he wrapped his hand around his cock. She probably wouldn't come back tonight. He began to stroke his needy shaft, hungering for release more than he ever had in his life.

Dana headed to her room and reluctantly showered, unhappy at washing off Mason's scent from her body, then put on her pajamas. She climbed into bed, cuddling his robe in her arms. She debated whether to go back to his room and sleep on his couch, but if she went back, she was afraid she wouldn't be able to resist climbing into bed with him again. But that might make him angry and ruin the progress she'd made.

What they had done together had been pure bliss! He made her feel things she'd never experienced. She'd given herself orgasms before, but nothing like that. His touch was pure heaven.

But where they were was fragile right now, so she should probably stay right here and give him a little space. She snuggled her face into his robe, breathing in his masculine scent.

At his reaction to her wearing the maid's uniform tonight, she'd feared it had been a big mistake, but in the end, it had taken them further than she'd gotten with him until now. She just wished it hadn't made him angry. She didn't want to take any chance on pushing him away. She hadn't known he'd be touchy about it. Surely, he didn't know that she knew about the incident.

She couldn't believe how she'd flung the costume off

at his command. She hadn't done it to be seductive. But when he'd commanded her to take it off, she'd responded without thought. As if she were programmed to do whatever he told her to do. It was so strange.

And incredibly sexy.

She was just glad the apron had covered her tattoo. She would have died of embarrassment if he had seen it. Why she'd thought she'd be able to get away with having sex with him without him seeing it, she didn't know, but she never thought about him actually staring at her down there so closely. Of course, if they went through with it, he would see it at some point. She just couldn't cope with it tonight. She smiled as she remembered how much of a gentleman he'd been about it.

She rolled over, wanting to sleep, but unable to stop thinking about him stretched out in his bed, sexy as hell, in the next room.

Dana woke up to the vibration of her phone. She opened her eyes and stared at the ceiling above her. The familiar, stucco ceiling of Mason's room.

She smiled. She had crept back into his room last night after all and now she peered over the back of the couch to see him.

And her jaw dropped. Oh, God, he was totally naked, his cock standing straight up. Just like that morning so many years ago.

She stood up and walked toward the bed, like a paper clip drawn to a magnet. A big, hard, iron rod of a magnet.

She knelt beside his bed and simply stared at his huge member, wanting to reach out and touch it.

He murmured sleepily and his head turned. In the old days, she would've fled, ensuring that he didn't see her, but this time, she just continued to kneel there, looking at him. His eyelids fluttered open and he gazed at her. Then he seemed to realize that he was lying naked in full view of her and he grabbed for the covers.

"No, please. Don't," she said.

He hesitated. "Dana . . ."

"What's wrong with me looking at you? I like seeing your big . . . uh . . . penis."

His lips turned up. "Looking at it. You can barely say it."

"Penis," she said more confidently. "Cock. *Erection.*" She smiled. "See. I can say it just fine."

"So you can."

Mason watched her. Her look of awe as she gazed at his cock filled him with heat.

"I want to touch it."

"I don't think that's a good idea, Dana."

"I think it's a *very* good idea." Her gaze shifted to his. "Please."

He sighed. Fuck, what was he going to say? The thought of her soft touch on his hard flesh made him harden even more.

When he didn't say anything, she reached for him tentatively. At the first brush of her soft fingers, he sucked in a breath.

"Did I hurt it?" She bit her lower lip, her fingers hovering near his aching cock as she gazed at his face.

"No, that wasn't pain, baby."

"Oh." Then she smiled and, God help him, she wrapped both hands around his shaft. Her soft fingers began to glide up and down. Very lightly.

"You're so big. I can't even wrap my fingers all the way around you." Her wide eyes shifted from his member back to his eyes. "Are all men this big?"

He smiled. "Well, I don't want to brag."

"Oh." Then she laughed. A delightful, melodic sound.

She wrapped one hand around him as best she could, then she stroked his length with the fingertips of her other hand.

"What do you like? How do you want me to touch you?"

"That's good. *Really* good. And stroking it up and down."

"I can do that." She stared at his shaft with great interest, then wrapped both hands around him again—one over the other—and began to stroke him, gliding over his hot, needy flesh. After several strokes, she stopped and ran her finger over his tip, sending need vibrating through him.

"What about the top? Is it sensitive?"

"Oh, yeah. Especially under the crown."

"You mean here?" She ran her fingertip under the mushroom tip, circling around.

"Yeah, baby. That's perfect."

She smiled at his praise. She released him for a moment and climbed onto the bed, sitting with her legs to the side. She leaned toward him and her tongue flicked out, licking his tip.

"Fuck, Dana, what are you doing?"

"I know that men like it when a woman takes him in her mouth." Then she opened and wrapped her lips around his tip. Her tongue flickered over him as she pressed her mouth down, taking more of him inside her moistness.

"Dana, you don't need to—"

Her mouth captured his entire cockhead, and she squeezed. Intense need thrummed through him.

"Oh, God, Dana."

Her eyes glittered as she gazed up at him and, if her mouth hadn't been full of his cock, he was sure she'd be smiling from ear to ear.

Then she glided deeper on him, taking his shaft in her hot mouth, too.

What she did next knocked his socks off. He saw her throat move as if she were swallowing, and the suction on his cock felt incredible.

"Oh, fuck, baby. How did you learn that?"

She pulled his big cock from her mouth like a lollipop and licked it. "I read about oral sex in a magazine, and this article said to swallow and it'll cause a lot of suction. You liked it, didn't you?"

"Fuck, are you kidding?" He stroked her cheek. "Please, just do it again."

She giggled, then her hot mouth surrounded him and she did it again.

But, damn it, it felt so good he was going to blow any second.

"Baby, no, stop. I'm going to—"

She released him again, still holding him tightly in her soft hands. "I want you to come in my mouth. Don't say you won't. Men like that, I know. And . . ." She gazed straight into his eyes. "I want to do that. I want to feel you come in my mouth."

She swallowed him and sucked, dragging intense pleasure from him with every pulse of her mouth. Her delicate hands glided down his shaft, then she grazed his balls with her fingertips. When she cupped them in her hand and caressed, he felt himself losing it. She did that super-suction thing again, still cradling his balls in her palm, and he felt it.

His balls tensed and his groin burned as the pressure built. Then it happened. He erupted into her like a full-scale volcano, filling her sweet mouth with his hot semen.

She swallowed, causing more suction, as he continued to stream into her, groaning at the intense pleasure she gave him. Then she swallowed again.

When he was finished, she slid her mouth from his hot cock. Then she licked it, swirling her tongue over the tip and down around the shaft.

Damn, it was so sexy that his waning erection swelled

again. He wanted to drag her onto the bed and drive into her sweet naked little pussy.

He pulled her close, loving her soft body so tight against him. He captured her mouth, rolling her over and tucking her body beneath his. He nuzzled her neck, loving her soft whimpers of pleasure.

"Oh, Mason, I want you."

And he wanted her. Fuck, so much.

He slid her loose pajama top upward. His cock swelled as more of her creamy skin was exposed. Then he revealed her breasts, so round and lovely, and his cock ached for her. He gazed at them in awe, then caressed them. Her nipples tightened in his hands and he stroked the tiny tips with his fingers, watching them pebble.

He licked one, and she moaned softly.

"Oh, baby, you are so sweet."

He couldn't stand it. He needed to see all of her. He grabbed the elastic on her pajama pants and pulled them down, then tossed them aside.

Oh, God, she was beautiful.

Then his gaze fell on her left hip.

Her eyes widened. "Oh!"

He grinned and stroked her tattoo. The word "Courage" written in script at an angle on her pelvis, just a breath away from her pussy.

"Now what's this?" he asked as he stroked along the text with his fingertip.

"I . . . uh . . ." She looked panicky.

"What a coincidence. I have one just like this on my ass." He leaned down and kissed the tattoo, then lightly brushed his lips in butterfly kisses along its length. "Almost makes me think you were spying on me in the shower." He nuzzled the flesh beside her tattoo, his lips brushing the outer side of her soft folds. "Did my naughty little stepsister spy on me?"

She squirmed under him, looking so uncomfortable he took pity on her and covered her pussy with his mouth, scattering any thoughts either of them had on the subject of the tattoo. As he sank his tongue into her, all he could think about was tasting her. He licked the length of her and she widened her legs to give him better access.

He nuzzled her soft, wet flesh, smiling at the silky warm feel of her in his mouth. God, it was like he'd died and gone to heaven.

But his cock twitched, demanding more. He wanted to be inside her body.

He suckled her small bud and she moaned.

Then as if reading his thoughts, she tightened her fingers around his shoulders and said, "Oh, Mason, please don't make me wait any longer. I want to feel you inside of me."

He wanted to so badly, but he wouldn't. Not with his cock, anyway.

Yesterday, he hadn't pressed his fingers inside her, not wanting to breach her untouched opening, but now, he glided a finger inside her and stroked her velvety channel. God, she was so inviting. His cock swelled even bigger.

He glided another finger into her as he licked her folds.

"Baby, do you like that?" he asked, though her arching body told him she did.

"Oh, yes." She squeezed his shoulders again. "But I want more."

"We need to take it slow. You're tight. Be patient."

He glided his fingers into her, slowly. In and out. She was tight and her passage gripped his fingers snugly. He kissed her folds as he continued to slide his fingers in and out, then he stroked her inner channel, finding the G-spot. She gasped and arched against him. He kept stroking it as he began to suckle her clit. She became frantic, arching against him, tossing her head side to side.

He glided his fingers deeper, fucking her gently and wishing it were his cock inside her.

"Oh, Mason." Her fingers glided to his head and she threaded her fingers through his hair, holding him to her. Then she arched and moaned.

"Come for me, baby."

"Yes." She gasped. "Oh, yes!!!" Then she wailed her release, her sweet voice filling the room.

He kept plunging his fingers into her, within the softness of her warm body, as he teased her clit, keeping her orgasm going and going.

Finally, she collapsed on the bed, gasping for air.

He smiled down at her, loving the blissful glow beaming from her face. She gazed up at him and his breath caught at her beauty. He wiped his face, then leaned down and kissed her. Her arms tightened around his neck and her lips found his. Her tongue dipped into his mouth and undulated against his.

"Oh, that was so good." She smiled tremulously up at him and his heart toppled.

God, she was perfect.

As Mason and Dana sat eating breakfast together, still in his suite, Dana seemed quiet.

Mason sipped his coffee, then put down the cup. "Is there something wrong, Dana?"

She pushed her eggs around her plate, then put her fork down. "What we did this morning was . . . um . . . really special, but you seem to be avoiding actually . . . uh . . ."

"Taking your virginity?"

She nodded. "That's right." She picked up her fork and pushed her eggs around again. "I'm just wondering if . . . well . . ." She put down her fork again. "Is there something wrong with me?"

"Wrong with you? Of course not. Why would you think that?"

She pursed her lips. "Well, you won't actually . . . you know . . . make love to me."

"Dana, just give it more time. I don't want to rush this."

He'd have to talk to her about this sooner or later, but not right this minute.

"I just . . . I always wondered if there was something about me."

He raised an eyebrow. "Why?"

"Well, you left when I was eighteen. Without even a word of good-bye. Without ever contacting me again."

She frowned and the sadness in her eyes filled him with pain.

"Why *did* you leave, Mason?"

He stared at her, his heart clenching. How could he possibly answer that question?

Part Two

Mason reached out and stroked her cheek, his chest tight. "Dana, believe me, there is nothing wrong with you. You are perfect."

That caused her lips to turn up a little.

He wanted to tell her that his leaving had nothing to do with her, but that would be a lie. He couldn't even say it wasn't because of something she'd done.

He knew she suspected that he'd left because of her obvious attraction to him, but that wasn't true. If he told her the real reason, though, she would blame herself, and he didn't want that.

She pursed her lips. "You aren't going to tell me, are you?"

"No." He took her delicate hand in his. "I'm sorry I abandoned you. I wish it could have been otherwise, but it is the way it is, so can we put it behind us?"

"I thought you hated me," she said, clearly fighting

back tears. "I thought I'd done something wrong and you needed to get away from me." Her voice caught. "Or you just didn't care."

He squeezed her hand, his heart breaking at the emotional scars he'd caused her. "Oh, Dana, no. I have always cared about you. You believe me, don't you?"

She gazed at him, her eyes shimmering and his breath held.

Finally, she nodded. "I do now. The way you've been with me here. The fact that you cared enough to . . ." She sucked in a breath. "You looked out for me by buying my contract. And then agreed to . . . fulfill it."

Despite himself, he laughed. "Fulfill it? Why, Dana, you're so romantic."

She dashed away an errant tear, then began to laugh. "Yes, well . . . I suppose there hasn't really been much romance in my life." She leaned her chin on her hand. "I mean, think about it. I didn't even lose my virginity at my prom like most of my friends did."

He tipped his head. "Yeah, what about that? You *were* out all night."

She pursed her lips. "Let's just say you have secrets about the past, and so do I."

But he saw a flash of pain in her eyes and his hands balled into fists under the table. He didn't know what that jerk had done to hurt her, but if Mason ever got his hands on him, he'd pummel the truth out of him.

He drew in a deep breath and brought his attention

back to Dana. "You know, I can't do anything about the past, but I could do something about that lack of romance."

"Like what?"

"Like take you out on the town. We could get all dressed up and go out to dinner and dancing. What do you say?"

"Tonight?"

"Sure, why not? There's a dinner-and-dance cruise along the river. You can put on a glamorous dress and I'll wear my best suit."

She smiled. "I like that idea. Maybe even a tux?" She ran her hand along the lapel of his robe. "You'd look very handsome in a tuxedo."

He raised an eyebrow. "And I wouldn't in a tailored, designer suit?"

She laughed. "You look devastatingly gorgeous in old blue jeans, so stop fishing for compliments."

Once they finished breakfast, she helped him clear the dishes off the table.

"I need to get some reading done for classes," she said. "I don't want to fall too far behind."

He had set their two weeks together over her reading week at school, but that was only one week, so she was losing one week of classes.

"That's fine. I have some things I need to follow up on, including arrangements to make for tonight."

Her face lit up as she smiled, and he smiled back. He wished he could keep her smiling like that forever.

•   •   •

Dana entered her suite and walked to the desk in the study area. She pulled out her French literature textbook and started reading the chapters assigned for this week. But soon her mind wandered.

Mason was taking her out dancing tonight. What would she wear? He'd said she could put on a glamorous dress and he'd wear a suit, but she didn't really have anything fancy enough. As a student, she didn't need dressy outfits. She did have a little black dress. Her mom had always insisted she own a little black dress, and that she pack it whenever she went anywhere. The habit had stayed with her. She also had the pearls her father had given her. They'd been her grandmother's, so she cherished them. But a black dress and pearls wasn't really her style.

She was tempted to skip out on studying and go shopping instead. To buy a stunning gown that would dazzle Mason. She opened her computer and searched several stores online to get some ideas. She found some stunning gowns on the website of an upscale department store that was nearby, but the prices were far beyond her budget.

Someone knocked on her door.

"Come in," she called.

The door opened and Mason stepped inside.

"Hi. I know you're busy, but can I interrupt for a minute?" he asked.

"Sure."

He walked to her desk and settled in the guest chair.

"I wanted to let you know that all the arrangements have been made for tonight. We leave at six o'clock."

"Okay, great."

"And right now, I'm going into town. Is there anything you'd like me to pick up? Or are you up for a break? We could grab lunch together."

She bit her lip and glanced at the beautiful gowns on the screen, reconsidering whether she should go and buy one. But she knew she couldn't afford it.

"No, I really can't take the time."

He nodded, but seemed reluctant to leave just yet.

"So what are you working on? An essay?"

She shook her head, and started to close the browser.

He peered around at her screen and chuckled. "Looking at dresses. I should have known." Suddenly his face grew serious. "Dana, do you have a nice dress here that you can wear tonight?"

"Well, I . . . uh . . . I'm sure I have something."

He furrowed his brow. "You don't, do you?"

He took her hand and drew her to her feet. "That settles it. You're coming into town with me and I'm buying you a new dress. Shoes and jewelry, too."

She drew her hand away. "No."

His gaze locked with hers. "Why not?"

"I . . ." She shook her head. "I just don't want you spending money on me, that's all."

"Why not? I've got lots of money. It doesn't bother me. Why should it bother you?"

She crossed her arms.

"Uh oh. Your stubborn look." His eyes glittered with amusement.

He rested his hands on her shoulders, which sent tremors through her, throwing her totally off-balance. His effect on her was palpable, but he remained calm and collected, as though he wasn't aware of it at all.

"Dana, I wish you'd let me do this for you. I want to take you on a magical night." He smiled. "Romance, remember?"

"Mason, it doesn't matter what I wear. Just being with you will make it magical."

He laughed. "That's very charming, and I love that you think that way, but we still have to meet the dress code. The cruise is formal."

"Don't worry. I will meet you downstairs at six sharp, dressed appropriately. Okay?"

"Good." He glanced at her laptop, the screen dark. "So are you going to get some good work done while I'm gone, or are you just going to goof off?"

She laughed. "I didn't get through three years of college by goofing off."

He smiled warmly. "I know you didn't." He leaned forward and kissed her cheek. "I'll see you at six."

He turned and walked across the room, then disappeared out the door.

As soon as he was gone, she bit her lip, the desire to be dazzling for him tempting her beyond reason. She walked to the window and watched the limousine pull up out front and Mason get inside.

Should she run down and tell him she'd changed her mind?

She wanted him to stare up at her in adoration when she walked down the stairs this evening.

Suddenly, images of the one time in real life when exactly that had happened flashed through her mind. He had watched her descend the stairs with rapt attention, as if she were the most beautiful woman in the world. What had happened after that . . . her chest constricted. She wouldn't think about that now.

She wrung her hands. But maybe . . . just maybe . . . She raced across the room and pulled open her closet door, then peered at the top shelf.

"Oh, my God. It's still here."

Mason stood in the entryway and glanced at his watch. He'd knocked on Dana's door ten minutes ago and she'd called out that she'd meet him downstairs on time. But her idea of "on time" and his had often differed.

Then he heard footsteps on the hardwood floor of the upstairs hallway. He glanced up and sucked in a breath. There she stood, with a glowing smile on her face, just as beautiful in that frothy pink gown as the first time he'd seen her in it.

His chest constricted as the painful memories surrounding that night seared through him. What had happened then had set in motion a catastrophic series of events.

Radiant in a gown that seemed made just for her, Dana

was oblivious to his pain. And the sight of her in that dress still made his body harden with need.

Eight Years Earlier on Prom Night
Mason watched eighteen-year-old Dana walk down the grand staircase, glowing like a new bride in her sweet, almost-virginal pastel-pink prom gown. Her hair was swept up in a sophisticated French twist, with delicate, wispy curls fluttering around her face and shoulders.

She looked like a beautiful fairy princess, but despite the sweetness of the image, the way the fitted bodice accentuated her tiny waist and full, round breasts, and the way those breasts swelled from the strapless gown, made him long to peel it away and caress the silken flesh underneath. As she walked down the stairs, beaming, his groin tightened. He wanted to sweep her into his arms and seduce her with passionate kisses. Then carry her to his bed and ravage every inch of her sweet, innocent body.

But it was not to be. He was her stepbrother, not her lover.

A protectiveness surged through him as he thought about how Geoffrey Miller would be picking Dana up in a few minutes and then later, after the dance, his meaty paws would be all over her.

Just like a virgin bride on her wedding day, she would be divested of her innocence. He just wished it could be with someone who would take it slow. Who would ensure she experienced a blissful first time.

He wished it could be him.

"What do you think?" she asked, her cheeks tinged pink.

He smiled. "You look stunning."

She smiled so broadly, he would swear that his compliment was the most important thing in the world to her. He knew she valued his opinion and that it boosted her confidence. Aside from her real father, whom she hardly ever saw, Mason was the only positive male influence in her life. His father paid no attention to her, except the odd leering flicker of interest when she and her mother weren't looking, which sickened Mason.

Dana threw herself into his arms, wrapping hers around his neck. Then she pushed up on her toes and kissed him. Her lips were soft on his and, fuck, her sweet little tongue pushed between his lips and into his mouth. Soft and velvety. Without thinking, he opened, then swept his tongue into her mouth. She mewed softly, melting against his body, her soft breasts crushed against him.

Damn, this was a heaven he was not meant to experience. His cock swelled at the feel of her so close. Gripped by a need so intense he could barely breathe, he pulled her tight to his body.

Then, fuck, she rocked her hips forward. She had to feel his hot, hard arousal against her. And it seemed to excite her because she pulled him closer and thrust her tongue deeper into his mouth.

He pulled his lips away, gazing down at her large,

dewy eyes, filled with a heat that triggered a yearning so deep inside him that he could barely stop himself from pressing her back against the nearest wall and burrowing under her voluminous skirt to find the sweet, damp prize beneath. Then driving his rock-hard erection deep inside her. He longed to feel the divine delight of her warm, intimate channel embracing his hot, hard steel.

Right at this moment, he knew she would let him sweep her away to his bedroom and take everything she had to offer. Her innocent, nubile body could be his for the taking.

The doorbell rang.

Fuck, what the hell was he thinking? He couldn't do that. She was his stepsister. And she trusted him to protect her. He had been so close to betraying that trust.

The doorbell rang again and he had to wrap his hands around her shoulders—her soft, bare skin in his grip disconcerting—and ease her away.

"That's your date," he murmured. "It's time to go."

"But, I thought . . ."

Her wide eyes filled with disappointment. And the pain of rejection. Damn it.

He could hear the butler's footsteps approaching the entrance.

"You look beautiful." Mason smiled. "If you didn't have a date, I might be tempted to sweep you away," he said in a light tone, trying to buoy her shattered confidence, "but you have Geoff waiting for you. So go and have a wonderful time."

As Mason and Dana stood talking at the foot of the staircase in the large foyer, Mason's back to the entrance, the butler arrived and opened the door.

Dana's lower lip quivered. Mason kissed her cheek, then turned and smiled at the young man standing in the doorway in his tailored tuxedo, an orchid boutonniere on his lapel.

"Good evening, Geoff," Mason said.

But Geoff's gaze was on Dana, soaking in her breathtaking beauty.

"You look beautiful, Dana," he said.

Jealousy surged through Mason, knowing this oaf would deflower his innocent Dana this evening. But he kept a steel grip on his emotions and smiled. He watched as the boy handed Dana the orchid corsage he'd brought for her, matching the flower he wore. Luckily, it was a wrist corsage so Mason didn't have to suffer watching Geoff fumble with putting it on her. The thought of Geoff's fingers brushing against the swell of her breasts as he pinned through the delicate fabric would have driven Mason crazy.

"Good evening, sir," Geoff said, then took Dana's hand and led her to the door.

Damn. The "sir" made him feel like Dana's father rather than her stepbrother, and made their age difference seem to broaden.

Finally, the door closed behind them and Mason was left standing alone in the cavernous foyer.

"Well, wasn't that just a sickening sight."

He turned to see Maria, one of the maids, standing
behind him. She was cheeky and impertinent, at least when
his father and stepmother weren't around. And he suspected she was having an affair with his father. That would
explain how she got away with her behavior. Not that
Mason gave a damn. He didn't care for formality with the
servants. He preferred a more casual relationship with
those that worked for him, but Maria carried it a little far.

"Why didn't you just drag the brat upstairs and drill
her? You've wanted to ever since you returned to this
house."

"Shut up, Maria." He turned and strode toward the
den at the back of the house.

She followed him. He took off his suit jacket and
dropped it over the back of the leather desk chair, then
poured himself a scotch and threw it back.

She grinned and walked toward him. "You know, I
saw the way you kissed her. That was no brotherly kiss. I
was surprised you didn't pull up the brat's skirt and fuck
her against the wall. Or did her date arrive just a little too
soon?"

"Maria, don't talk that way about Dana."

She laughed. "I wasn't talking about Dana. I was talking about you."

She stepped close and gazed at his pants. His fucking
hard-on was still alive and well, and visible now that he'd
shed his jacket.

"You know, I could help you with that."

"Don't you have work to do?"

She smiled. "Actually, no. I'm on a break." She moved close to him and stroked her hand over his hip, a breath away from his aching erection.

Ordinarily, he would push her hand away. He didn't like sexually aggressive servants like Maria, who slept with the men in the house for special favors. Maria had probably been screwing his father for years, and she had definitely pursued Mason since he'd returned, too. He'd always flatly turned her down. But now, with his cock aching for Dana, and his head filled with thoughts of another man touching her, he needed a distraction.

He poured himself another drink.

And why the fuck not? He was an adult. And a man. If Maria wanted to give away what he so sorely needed right now, then why the hell not?

Encouraged, Maria stepped closer. Her hand stroked over his bulging erection, her fingers wrapping around it. Then her eyes widened.

"Oh, my God, you are *big*."

"Bigger than my father?" he asked, tipping back his glass again.

She shrugged. "How would I know?"

She squeezed him, then unzipped his pants and pulled him out. The feel of her fingers around his aching flesh sent a flood of heat rushing through him.

"You've really got it bad for that little brat, don't you?" she said, staring at his throbbing cock.

"Don't talk about her like that."

She grinned. "Of course, sir." Then she sank to her knees, stroking his stomach. "Let me take your mind off her."

Her lips wrapped around his cockhead and he groaned.

She bobbed up and down on him, her mouth hot and moist, then she took him deep down her throat. Heat pulsed through him. He tipped back his glass, then thumped it down on the table.

She squeezed him in her mouth, driving his need higher.

Then her warm mouth slid away and she stood up. She began unbuttoning her black uniform. He watched her fingers move to each button and release it in turn, slowly revealing the swell of her bosom. His cock twitched, hard and needy.

When she got to her waist, she reached around and untied her apron, letting it flutter to the ground. Then she continued unbuttoning the dress until it fell open. Underneath, she wore lacy black lingerie, including garters and black stockings. Probably at the instruction of his father.

She smiled, then slid her thumbs under the waistband of her panties and pushed them down, revealing her pussy, shaven, except for a patch of curls in the shape of a heart. She had a tattoo to the left of it: C T. His father's initials.

"Do you like what you see?" she asked, as she opened the dress wider. Then her hand stroked down her belly and between her legs. "I'm so wet for you."

"Fuck, Maria, why are you doing this?"

She walked toward him and pressed her hands against his chest. Then she stroked.

"I want to help you forget about her." She nuzzled his neck, sending tingles through him. "I know how hard you struggle with it."

She wrapped her arms around him and lifted her face to his, then captured his mouth. Her lips were soft and coaxing. But they weren't Dana's.

Desire blasted through him. For Dana. To be with her. But he couldn't have that. So he dragged Maria against him, and ravaged her mouth, driving his tongue deep. Plundering. When he released her mouth, she was panting.

"Oh, yeah. I like that," she gasped. Then she clutched his shoulders. "Take me."

His blood boiled with need. He backed Maria up against the wall, then slid his hands up her sides and over her breasts. They were full and round, fitting his palms. He squeezed.

She ran a finger down his chest. "If you want, you could take me from behind. Then you could pretend my tight hole is her little virgin passage."

Ah, fuck. He scowled and started to back away.

When she saw she was losing him, she pulled the cups of her bra down, revealing her tight, hard nipples. He froze, his groin aching.

"Okay, never mind her. But finish what we've started

here." She grabbed his wrist and drew him closer, then pressed his hands against her naked breasts and squeezed. "I want you to take me as if it were against my will." Her eyes glowed with need. "As if you're forcing me." She grabbed his hard cock and squeezed. "That turns me on so much."

He hesitated, the heat of her hard nipples burning into his palms.

She stroked his hard, aching cock. "I'll protest, but drive it into me hard," she whispered. "I like that."

Fuck, kinky bitch. Hormones flooded him.

He shoved her hard against the wall with a growl.

"Open your legs, bitch," he demanded.

"Yes, call me nasty names," she whispered against his ear as she widened her legs. But aloud, she said, "No, sir. Please don't."

He grasped his hard shaft and pressed it to her pussy, then glided the tip over her slick flesh.

Desperately needing to be inside her, he positioned his cock against her opening, to her quiet murmurs of approval.

"Oh, sir, we shouldn't." She pressed her hands against his chest and began to struggle against him.

Every time she called him "sir," his blood boiled. He'd never experienced anything like it.

He thrust into her, driving deep. He groaned, his cock now buried in her to the hilt. Damn, the feel of her hot moistness around him nearly drove him mad with lust.

"Ohhhh," she moaned.

He drew back and drove into her again.

Her hands curled around his shoulders and she pushed against him. "Oh, sir. No."

He gazed at her eyes and the heat there assured him she wanted this.

"Fucking slut," he berated. "I'm going to fuck you so hard, you'll feel it into next week."

He grabbed her wrists and pressed them against the wall above her head and thrust again. Oh, God, she was so hot and warm around him.

She struggled against him as he kept driving into her, but passion and need filled her eyes.

He pounded her against the wall, filling her again and again. Her cries filled the room, but he knew no one else would hear. The butler was polishing silver in the dining room on the other side of the house, and Maria was the only other servant on at this time of the evening.

Her whimpers and the moist, hot grip of her body around his swelling cock sent pleasure thundering through him.

"I'm going to come," she murmured against his ear.

He drove harder and faster, then felt his own pleasure building. She wailed her release in his ear, her orgasm causing her pussy to spasm around him.

"Fuck," he groaned. His balls tightened and his cock exploded inside her. He drove her hard against the wall,

then pinned her there as the intense release of his body
filled him with overwhelming pleasure.

She wasn't Dana, but she was what he'd needed. A soft,
warm woman to fuck hard and fast to relieve his desperate yearning.

But now, with his cock still buried inside her, he felt
disgust. Why the fuck had he succumbed to Maria? She
was trouble and he didn't need any of that.

He pulled away, his cock sliding from her warm channel. He tucked it away and zipped up his pants.

"Your break must be over by now," he said in a dismissive tone. He wouldn't let her think this had been any
more than a one-time thing.

He turned and left the room, leaving her to pull herself together. As he walked up the stairs, he thought he
heard someone in the upstairs hallway, then a door close,
but that made no sense. Dad and Mason's stepmother were
on yet another trip and Dana was out.

That reminder of Dana in the hands of another man—
actually a mere boy—made him scowl. He retired to his
room.

Present Day

Dana watched Mason as she descended the stairs, feeling
like Cinderella in her full skirt and sequined pink high
heels. She wanted to race down the stairs and throw herself into his arms.

Earlier, as she'd pulled on the gown, she'd remem-

bered the feeling of rejection when Mason had sent her
on her way with her prom date eight years ago.

The way he'd looked at her as she'd come down the
stairs had filled her heart with hope that she could finally
convince him that they could be together. She'd been
eighteen, so legally an adult. And when she'd kissed him,
he'd seemed just as enamored with her as she'd been with
him. But then . . .

But she'd promised herself she wouldn't think of him
sending her away. And then what had happened afterward.

She reached the bottom of the stairs and smiled at him.
But he wasn't smiling back. She had hoped to see the same
longing in his eyes tonight as she had back then, because
now they were going to be together. There was no guess-
ing about that. But tonight he was even more withdrawn
than he had been then.

Oh, God, this had been a mistake. She sucked in a
deep breath, willing herself not to flee back up the stairs
and lock herself in her room.

Eight Years Earlier on Prom Night
Dana stepped outside with her hand on Geoff's elbow, and
the door closed behind them. She drew in a deep breath
of the evening air as he led her to the waiting limo, still
shaken by what had happened between her and Mason.

She'd kissed Mason with everything she had, allowing all her loving feelings free rein. Showing him just how
much she loved him.

And she'd felt it in the way he'd held her. In the way his lips had moved on hers, leaving her breathless and hungry.

The feel of his massive member growing so hard under his pants had both delighted and frightened her a little. But only because it felt so big and powerful. Mason was a grown man, and she was still so young.

But she'd wanted him with all her heart.

Then he'd just sent her away.

She'd felt sure he returned her feelings and she could finally tell him how much she longed for him. That she could take Mason's hand and lead him up to her bedroom, then surrender her virginity to him. Letting him guide her to womanhood. And, hopefully, beyond.

But Geoff had arrived and shattered that dream.

The driver opened the door of the limo and Geoff helped her inside. She sat in the leather seat and he sat beside her.

"You really do look beautiful tonight, Dana," he said.

"Thank you." When she glanced at him, the lust in his eyes was obvious and she realized he would be expecting her to put out at the end of the night. Or, with the increasing heat of his gaze, maybe even in the back of the limo on the way there.

No, she was being crazy. He wouldn't push her like that. But she knew he would expect it later . . . and why wouldn't he? Practically the only thing her girlfriends had talked about for the past month was how exciting it would be on prom night. And how it would be the perfect evening for giving themselves to their special dates.

But Geoff wasn't special to her. In fact, this was their first date. And the hungry look in his eyes only made her uncomfortable.

The limo started to move away from the curb and her heart leapt. The man she really wanted was in the house they were pulling away from. Of course he hadn't reacted to her kiss the way she'd hoped. She was dressed up for another man and they were interrupted by his knocking at the door.

So how could Mason possibly have realized what she really wanted?

Her heart pounded in her chest. She had to go back. She glanced at Geoff in a panic. She couldn't give him what he wanted, and it wouldn't be fair to make him think she would. If she cut their date short, she knew he'd find someone else to fulfill his fantasy for tonight. All the girls wanted Geoff, the school's star athlete. He could have his pick.

"Geoff?" She grasped his arm.

"What is it, Dana?"

"I'm sorry but . . . I have to go back."

"Did you forget something?"

She shook her head. "I'm . . . I'm not feeling well."

He frowned, and she was sure he was going to protest.

"I think . . ." She covered her mouth with her hand. "I think I might throw up. It must be something I ate."

"Oh, damn, don't throw up." He knocked on the window between them and the driver, and the driver lowered the glass. "Take us back to Dana's house."

Dana kept her hand over her mouth as they pulled up in front of the entrance.

"I'm so sorry, Geoff. Really."

He frowned, but nodded. As she closed the door behind her, she could see Geoff pulling out his cell phone, probably to call another girl to replace her. The car pulled away, leaving her on the doorstep.

She walked up the stately stone steps and opened the door, then went inside. She sucked in a deep breath, gathering the courage to find Mason and tell him exactly how she felt about him. She would convince him that they could be together, then take his hand and lead him to her bedroom. Once the door closed behind them, they would both succumb to the passionate attraction between them.

She glanced up the stairs, wondering if he'd gone to his room. But then she saw a light at the end of the hallway, coming from the den. She smiled. He must be in there.

She slipped off her shoes, not wanting the clack of her heels on the hardwood to alert him to her presence. She wanted to see the surprise on his face when she appeared in the doorway. Then she would lock gazes with him as she walked toward him, feeling his adoring stare on her just like she had when he'd first seen her in her prom dress. It had been an amazing feeling, his intense blue eyes staring at her in awe as she'd descended the staircase.

She wanted to feel that again. She wanted to step into his den, then captivate him with her smile. He would say her name in his deep, sexy voice, then stand up and stride toward her, his eyes glittering as he approached. Then he'd take her in his arms and kiss her passionately, and tell her how happy he was she'd come back to him. She'd confess her love and he would sweep her into his arms and race up the stairs to her bedroom.

She sighed at the images swirling through her head as she crept along the hallway.

As she approached the den—her cheeks flushed with excitement at what she was about to do—she thought she heard noises coming from inside. Was someone in there with him? She thought she heard the low murmur of a woman's voice, then Mason's.

She crept closer to the door.

Then a moan.

Dana bit her lip as she peered through the partially open door.

"No, sir. Please don't," a woman cried.

Dana's eyes widened at the sight of one of the maids— she thought it was Maria—against the wall, with Mason's body crushed against her.

Dana's heart clenched and she wanted to jerk away, but she was mesmerized. What was Mason doing?

"Oh, sir, we shouldn't." Maria pressed her hands against his chest and began to struggle against him.

Then he thrust forward.

Dana's hands covered her mouth, stopping herself from gasping.

Mason was . . . Oh, God . . . he and Maria were . . .

She felt faint.

"Ohhhh," Maria moaned.

His hips drew back, then he drove into her again.

Maria's hands clutched his shoulders and she pushed against him. "Oh, sir. No."

Was Mason taking her against her will?

"Fucking slut," he barked. "I'm going to fuck you so hard, you'll feel it into next week."

He jerked her arms over her head and held them there.

Horrified, Dana watched as the woman struggled against him, protesting, but he kept driving into her. Dana began to tremble, torn between running to her room and running to get help. But she couldn't believe that Mason . . . that he would . . .

Mason pounded Maria against the wall, again and again. Her cries filled the room, but confusion spiraled through Dana as she realized that Maria's face was contorted in pleasure, not distress.

"I'm going to come," Maria whimpered.

Mason thrust harder and faster, and Maria wailed loudly.

"Fuck," he groaned, then drove her hard against the wall, pinning her there as his body shuddered.

Dana stood there, trembling. Oh, God, she couldn't believe what she'd just seen. Mason wasn't the kind of man to take a woman against her will. And rather than looking upset or panicked as Mason drew back, Maria smiled with a smug look of satisfaction on her face.

Dana didn't understand any of this.

Mason straightened his clothes and stepped back.

"Your break must be over by now," he said in a dismissive tone. Then he turned toward the door.

Oh, God, she couldn't let him see her. Dana raced up the stairs, already hearing Mason's footsteps in the hallway. She hurried along the upstairs hall to her door, her heart pounding. As she tapped in the combination to her door, her heart stopped as she realized he was on the stairs now. She got the last number wrong and it didn't unlock.

Oh, God, he was getting closer. He would soon be at the top of the staircase, then he'd see her.

She jabbed in the combination again and this time, the door unlocked and she slipped inside, tugging her full skirt in with her. She closed the door quietly behind her, then leaned against it, trying to catch her breath. Seconds later, his footsteps passed by her door.

She didn't think he'd seen her, but she waited there, praying he wouldn't knock on her door and demand she confess to spying on him.

Thankfully, she heard the thump of his door closing

and she released the breath she hadn't realized she'd been holding.

Finally, she calmed down enough to move, her legs still shaky. She dropped her pretty pink sequined shoes on the floor by her closet, then slumped onto the bed. Tears welled up in her eyes. Not only had her dream of finally confessing her love for Mason been stymied, but she'd seen him with another woman. A full-grown woman.

She'd been a fool to think Mason might be attracted to her. She was foolish and immature. He wanted a woman, not some naïve teenager.

She'd thought the evidence of his attraction to her when she'd kissed him had meant something, but it had just been a natural male reaction to a female body close to his. As soon as Dana had left the house, he'd found some-one to relieve that tension.

She realized now that he'd never been attracted to her and she had been a fool to think otherwise.

Her heart ached and her tears flowed freely. The pain was almost unbearable. She sobbed, wondering if she would ever recover from this dreadful agony. Moonlight washed across her cheek and she turned her face and buried it into the pillow.

Eventually she fell asleep, wondering how she would face Mason tomorrow.

Present Day

Dana stared at Mason, her stomach clenched at his stormy eyes.

"Why are you wearing that?" he asked her through gritted teeth. He almost seemed angry with her.

"Well, it was this or a little black dress with pearls and I didn't think you wanted to take out my mother."

"I told you I would have bought you a new dress."

She pursed her lips. "I know, and I appreciate that." She smoothed her hands down the side of the full skirt. "You're very generous. But I told you I'm not comfortable with you buying me things."

His hard gaze was still locked on her face.

She took his hand, loving the feel of his strong fingers within the grip of hers. "I thought you liked this dress," she murmured, longing for the look of adoration she had seen all those years ago when he'd first seen her in it. "You said you did on my prom night."

His eyes glittered, but he still frowned. "Of course I like the dress, Dana. It's perfect. You are absolutely beautiful in it."

She smiled at his compliment and stepped closer, her body mere inches from his. "You know, when I came down the stairs that night . . . and I saw you looking at me . . . I felt so . . ." She laughed softly, feeling her cheeks flush.

"You felt so what, Dana?" he prompted softly.

"I felt so beautiful." She gazed into his intense blue eyes, her cheeks heating. "So special."

He pulled her against him, his strong arms holding her close as his lips melded with hers. Her heart pounded in her chest, and when he released her mouth, she felt breathless.

"Special doesn't begin to describe you," he said. "You're the most beautiful woman I have ever seen."

She stared into his eyes, searching for the truth there. Was this real or just an attempt to boost her confidence? What she saw in the well of those midnight blue eyes was a depth of emotion that shocked her. She could almost believe she could see the love she felt for him, the love she had always denied until now, reflected back, but she knew that believing that would be her undoing.

All she could hope for would be that he would follow through on his promise to take her to womanhood, but once that played out, he would gently end things.

She would always treasure this time with him, but she was smart enough to know that it would only be a brief affair, one that was taboo and would be decreed by everyone—society, friends . . . family—as wrong.

He wouldn't want the kind of scandal that extending this relationship would bring to his life.

And her mother . . . Oh, God, she would be livid knowing Dana had anything to do with her ex-husband's family, let alone having an affair with his son.

Her stepbrother.

Dana couldn't imagine how her mother would react to her actually having a long-term, romantic relationship with him.

"Dana, the way you're looking at me . . . what do you think is going to happen between us?"

She cringed, wanting to back away. To catch her breath. But he still held her tight against his solid body.

"What we've agreed." She couldn't resist touching the satin lapels of his tuxedo. Her fingers glided along the smooth fabric. "You're going to . . ." Oh, God, she didn't want to say it aloud. It sounded so clinical saying he was going to take her virginity. "I mean, we'll spend some time getting to know each other again, then we're going to make love." Her lips turned up in a small smile. "Several times, I hope." When he didn't return the smile, hers faded. "And then I'll go back to school and continue my life. I'll go to Paris and pursue my master's with the money you are so generously giving me."

"So you're not expecting anything more as far as a relationship between us after these two weeks?"

"We're still family, sort of." She stroked her hands over his shoulders, the fine wool of his tuxedo smooth under her fingertips. "I'll always care about you." She frowned. "And being honest, I'll always wish we could have more, but I understand the problems that would cause, given our previous relationship as stepsiblings."

He nodded. "A very practical attitude."

She thought she read approval in his eyes, which both pleased her and made her heart sink. A part of her wished he would rage against her analysis, telling her they didn't need to live by society's rules. That if they wanted to be together, that's all that was important.

But that would mean that he did have the same feelings for her that she had for him, and that simply wasn't true. He was her protective older stepbrother, who cared about her, yes, but only in that context.

He didn't love her like she loved him.

She ran her fingertips under the collar of his tuxedo jacket, then down his lapels again. "So does that mean that tonight you will reward me with what I've been waiting for?"

"And what would that be?"

She locked gazes with him, letting him see the need in her eyes. "You know what I want, Mason. You've been teasing me with almost-there ever since we got here, but at some point I want you to fulfill your promise to be my first."

His arms loosened around her and she felt panic in the pit of her stomach.

"Dana, I need to be honest with you."

She drew in a deep breath. "Please," she said, happy her voice didn't shake.

"I brought you here hoping we would get to know each other better."

She nodded at his words.

"And my intent was that once you trusted me again, that I could talk you into taking the money without me following through on that deal."

Her chest constricted. "You . . . never intended to . . ." She blinked back a tear, her head shaking. "You really don't want me, do you?" God, her heart ached so badly.

He pressed his hand to the small of her back and pulled her tight to him again, then arched his pelvis toward her. A hard, thick bulge pressed against her, prominent despite layers of her full skirt between them. She gasped at the feel of it so hard against her.

"I want you, Dana. There is no doubt about that," he said, almost fiercely. "But that doesn't mean I should act on that desire. You're my stepsister."

"I am a grown woman," she retorted, just as fiercely. "And we're not stepsiblings. Our parents were married for less than three years a long time ago. I don't see why we should let that get in the way of what we want."

She ran her hand down his stomach, then wrapped her fingers around his thick bulge. She slid her hand up and down his engorged cock, feeling faint with the need to feel it inside her.

"You made a promise to me, and I expect that, as a gentleman, you will be true to that promise."

"Dana," he muttered through gritted teeth, his tone a warning. "You're playing with fire."

"Good, because I'm ready for a whole lot of heat." She found the tab of his zipper and glided it downward.

"Fuck." His hand slammed down on hers and he pulled it away, but then his lips were on hers, his tongue plunging into her.

He pulled her tighter to his muscular body, his arms around her, and if his tongue hadn't been exploring her mouth with such passion, she would have gasped at the feel of his long, impossibly thick cock pressed hard against her.

When he released her lips, she gazed at him, her eyes

wide. "Please, Mason. I need you so badly. I want to feel you inside me."

He groaned and she felt herself swept up into his arms. Then he was racing up the stairs with her, her heart pounding. He flung his door open and carried her inside.

Eight Years Ago

Mason parked his car in the garage, then walked into the house. It had been a tough week at work, pulling together a big deal to expand his company. Now he was looking forward to kicking back and watching a movie with Dana. She'd been looking forward to the new sci-fi thriller that had just come out on Blu-ray, and they had planned to watch it tonight.

As he walked down the hallway from the garage door entrance, he passed his father's study.

"Mason, I want to talk to you."

Mason frowned as he stopped at the doorway and peered into the study to see his father sitting at the desk.

"Not now, Dad. I have plans." Mason was long past doing as his father commanded. He had been for a long time.

"You will come in here and sit down right now. Do you understand?"

Mason simply turned and continued down the hall.

"It's about Dana."

Mason froze, his stomach clenching. He turned back and walked into the room. "Is she all right?"

His father gestured to the chair facing the desk. Mason

frowned, but sat down, knowing his father would use his weakness—Dana—against him. Chas would not be forthcoming with any more information until Mason did what he wanted.

Mason settled into the leather armchair and crossed his legs, keeping his composure despite his worry about Dana. Had something happened?

"Well?" he prompted.

"She's fine. She's gone away on a weekend trip with her mother."

Mason's eyebrows arched upward. In the whole time they'd all lived together, which had been close to two years, he had never seen that woman spend any quality time with her daughter. Now they had suddenly gone off on a trip together?

"What the hell's going on?" Mason demanded.

His father opened his desk drawer, then pulled out a brown envelope. He slid it across the glossy wood surface of the big desk toward Mason. Mason leaned forward and picked it up, then opened the envelope and pulled out the contents. It was a photograph and he stared at it with a frown. And a little shock.

It was a picture of him, naked, sporting a full erection. Sound asleep, it seemed.

He shoved it back in the envelope and tossed it on the desk.

"What the hell is this about? Have you put surveillance cameras in my room?"

Fuck, suddenly he wondered if his father knew about Dana sneaking into his room at night and sleeping on his couch.

"No, but maybe I should have." His father's hawk-like gaze bored into him.

"Then where the hell did you get this?" Mason demanded.

"We found *that,*" his father pointed a finger at the envelope, "on your sister's computer. Did you give her that photo?"

Mason scowled. "Of course not." He couldn't get his head around the fact that Dana had this picture. "How did you know it was on Dana's computer? You have no right to invade her privacy."

"Maria found it. She went into Dana's room to clean and Dana had left that on her computer screen." He shrugged. "Maria felt she had to let me know."

Mason scowled. "You're sticking with that story?" There were so many holes in it, he didn't know where to begin. The most obvious being that Dana would never leave a picture like that showing on her screen, and even if she had, the screensaver would have kicked in. Maria had to have been snooping.

"The bottom line is that I did find it. It doesn't matter how." He stared into Mason's eyes. "So you're screwing her?"

Mason glared at him. "Of course not. I would never do that."

"The picture suggests otherwise."

"You do see that I'm asleep in that picture?"

Chas shrugged. "Your eyes are closed. But no matter what you say, there is a picture of you, naked and fully aroused, on your younger sister's computer. She got it somehow." He crossed his arms. "And Maria has told me that more than once, she's seen Dana sneak out of your room first thing in the morning. Still in her pajamas."

"It was innocent," Mason said.

His father's eyebrows arched. "So you admit it."

Mason sighed. "I admit nothing, except to say that nothing has happened between Dana and me. How she somehow got a picture of me, asleep in my bed, I can't comment on, but there was nothing more to it."

His father pushed himself to his feet and walked around the desk, then picked up the envelope. "Do you know what this would do to our family if it got out?" he said, waving the envelope at him.

Mason stared at Chas stonily. "Well, it seems that it would only get out if you let it out."

Chas nodded and perched against the desk. "True. And, of course, I wouldn't do that."

He pulled the photo from the envelope again and dropped it on the desk in front of Mason. His gaze fell on Mason again, this time glittering with challenge. "But I should take it up with Dana."

Mason's gaze reluctantly fell on the photo. It was so damning, especially in the context of having been found in Dana's possession. He could just imagine Dana being faced with that photograph, presented by his father, probably with her mother present, and how mortified Dana would be.

She must have taken it one morning when she'd been sleeping on his couch—and God damn him for being so stupid as to sleep naked—but it was just a crazy mistake she'd made and she shouldn't be punished for it. And certainly not in such a horrifyingly embarrassing way. It would scar her.

Mason's eyes narrowed. "You don't need to do that."

"Oh, but I do. As her father, I need to protect her."

Mason stood up. "Fuck this. What will it take?"

His father turned to him; and thank God he didn't choose to pretend he didn't know what Mason was talking about.

"You will move out. Immediately. And you will have no contact whatsoever with Dana from now on."

Mason's heart clenched. Not only would that be painful for him, it would be devastating for Dana. He knew he gave her a stable influence in her life. She'd felt so alone all her life and he'd seen her blossom since the two of them had gotten close. Not that he had done anything more than someone who simply cared about her would do. But almost everyone else in her life, notably her mother, had failed miserably at giving her even a basic sense of being loved.

Could he really walk away from Dana without a word? Abandon her so completely?

But he knew his father would never let this drop. Even if Dana could get over the embarrassment of the photo, his father would find something else, and he would torture Dana as much as he could, especially knowing that she was Mason's weak spot.

Mason even wondered if Chas would leak the photo to the press, along with where it had been found, just to destroy Mason.

Chas had always been jealous of how well Mason did in business, and the fact that Mom had given Mason the money to start his own company, and he had been spectacularly successful, had pissed his father off to no end.

If Chas could destroy Mason's reputation, hoping to also destroy his success, then Mason fully believed he would do it, even if it caused him and his wife some embarrassment.

Mason had no doubt he could weather the scandal, but the real victim would be Dana and he would not allow his father's scheming to hurt her so viciously. So he made a split decision, as he'd been trained to do in business.

"All right, Chas. You win." He chose the words to give his father the satisfaction, knowing that's what his father's ego craved.

As Mason had grown up, Chas had struggled with Mason's achievements surpassing his own. In athletics, intelligence, and in business. His jealousy had been clear to both Mason and his mother.

Telling his father he won took nothing away from

Mason, but it gave him the great advantage that his father, now smug, would be easier to manipulate.

"I will leave, but I have a demand of my own."

"You're not in a position to demand anything, boy," his father snarled.

Mason stood up and walked toward Chas, like a panther stalking his prey. With a full five inches on him, Mason towered over his father.

"You will destroy the photo and never, *ever* tell Dana you knew about it. That goes for Maria, her mother, and anyone else who knows about it," he instructed. He took another step forward and his father took a step back. "And don't think that because I'm gone I won't be paying attention. If you hurt Dana—and believe me, I will know—I will destroy you." He glared at his father. An unwanted sense of satisfaction gleamed through him at the flicker of fear in his father's eyes. "I will destroy your business, and I will destroy *you*. And if you *ever*," Mason said the last word in a searing tone, his eyes flashing, "touch Dana . . ." At the mere thought a fury blasted through him that palpably increased the tension in the room. "I will kill you."

At that, he turned on his heel and strode away.

Present Day
Mason set Dana onto her feet, then swept her against him and devoured her mouth. Liquid fire blazed through his veins, and he was filled with the deep, blinding need to make love to her. He'd wanted her with a quiet despera-

tion for years, but he'd always been able to master that desire. But when she'd told him she needed him, and that
she wanted him inside her, he'd lost it.

His fingers found the metal tag of her zipper and he
slid it down. He eased back as the snug bodice loosened
from her body and fell away. She wore a dainty pink lace
bra, the same soft color as the gown, adorned with a smat-
tering of tiny pearls. It was strapless and held her beautiful
breasts up as though offering him their bounty.

She pushed the dress over her hips to the floor, revealing a pair of tiny panties that matched the bra. And, God
help him, she wore a matching garter belt with stockings.
Seeing her standing there in the erotic yet virginal-looking
lingerie and pink sequined spike heels that accentuated her
long, shapely legs, sent his heart stammering.

She smiled at his heated gaze and stepped close, then
drew him into her arms. She stroked his lapels, like she had
downstairs, setting his heart racing. Her lips brushed lightly
against his and he drew in a breath, then slid his arms
around her and pulled her closer. His tongue stroked the
seam of her lips and she opened for him, then he slid inside.
Her tongue met his and they danced an erotic rhythm together, undulating and curling around each other.

Her hands slid under his jacket and over his shoulders,
and he felt his jacket fall away. The delicate feel of her fingers releasing the buttons of his shirt sent quivers across
his flesh. Their lips parted and he pulled off his tie, then
tugged his shirt from his arms and shed it. Her hand glided

over his bulging cock, still restrained within his tuxedo pants. He unfastened the button and tugged down the zipper, desperate to feel her stroke his naked shaft with her delicate fingers.

They wrapped around him and he gasped. She gazed up at his face with a big smile, her face absolutely radiant.

But it was too fast. Too—

He sucked in a breath as she stroked him, flaming heat searing through him.

Too intense.

"Dana, wait," he said as he grasped her shoulders and pressed her back, far enough that her hand slipped from his throbbing member.

Her eyes widened in alarm. "Mason?"

"We have to—"

"No," she cried with determination and grabbed his shoulders. "I'm not going to let you change your mind. We both want this."

He couldn't help chuckling at her complete commitment to her goal. She was tenacious.

Her lips compressed. "Why are you laughing at me?"

Grinning, he shook his head, then kissed her lightly. "I'm not laughing at you. I was just going to say that we have to slow down. I'm a man, and I'm close to bursting with wanting you, so if you want me to take you gently, you'll have to work with me. Okay?"

The anxiety faded from her face and she smiled, a beautiful sight to behold.

"Oh." She nodded. "Of course. I'll do whatever you say. Just tell me what to do."

As strong as the fire already burning in him was, those words were like throwing gasoline on the flames. The Dom in him yearned to take complete control of her. To bend her to his will like a willow branch.

"Go grab a bottle of wine from the wine rack in the kitchenette and pour us each a glass. It will help us unwind a little."

As she followed his instructions, he pulled off his shoes, socks, and tuxedo pants, watching her performing the simple, domestic task wearing nothing but her lacy undergarments and high heels, his heart thudding in his chest.

She returned and offered him a glass of red wine. They clinked glasses and sipped. He knew that often the pain a virgin felt upon penetration was primarily because of anxiety, which caused the woman to tighten her internal muscles, so he wanted Dana to be as relaxed as possible. A glass of wine would help.

And making sure she was completely ready for him would also help.

Her gaze moved down his naked chest, over his abs, to his boxers, which were barely holding his swollen cock inside. She smiled and reached for him, but he captured her hand.

"What happened to me telling you what to do?"

She smiled impishly. "Well, you didn't tell me not to."

He grinned. "Okay. Don't touch."

She pouted, then sipped her wine. He led her to the bed and sat down with her beside him. His gaze locked on hers and hers dipped away, then returned as her cheeks blushed prettily.

God, she was so sweet and innocent. And all he wanted to do was push her down on the pristine white sheets and drive his aching cock inside her. To thrust into her until he heard her cry out in pleasure, and then gasp and moan his name as she shattered in orgasm.

Then he would erupt inside her, finally fulfilling the gut-wrenching yearning he'd suffered for over a decade.

But first, he had to ease them into things. Ensure it was a sweet and tender experience for her.

He didn't normally do either. Typically, the women he was with wanted to be handled roughly and with force. They wanted him to command them. Punish them. Completely dominate them.

And he'd come to need to do those things.

It had started with Maria on Dana's prom night, and continued for several months. Maria had kept him from going insane when he'd needed to release the agony of pent-up longing for Dana. He had found he enjoyed Maria's complete submission, and after his father had blackmailed Mason out of the mansion, and out of Dana's life, he'd found he'd developed a taste for submissive women. He'd tried vanilla relationships after that, but they just didn't satisfy him, so he sought out the type of women he needed.

He didn't know how long he could play the sweet lover, but he wanted Dana enough to subdue his dark urges and be what she needed right now. A gentle, tender lover.

"Should I pour us another?" Dana asked, holding up her empty glass.

He took the delicate crystal from her fingers and set it on the table beside the bed.

"No. No more wine." His lips spread into a smile. "I don't want anything to diminish your full enjoyment of what we're about to do."

He stroked her cheek, then glided his finger along the side of her neck. Her skin felt silky soft. He leaned forward and lightly brushed his lips against hers, then kissed the corner of her mouth. He fluttered kisses to her temple, then breathed softly into her ear. Her soft moan was a delight. He nuzzled her neck and she whimpered.

He eased back and allowed his gaze to travel over her body, lingering on her breasts. Her nipples pushed against the lace of her bra and he longed to set them free.

"Dana, you are so beautiful," he said, gliding his finger along her shoulder.

She watched him, her blue eyes wide.

He stroked downward, then dragged his fingertip along the edge of her lace bra, loving the silky feel of the swell of her breasts.

He reached around her and unfastened her bra, then drew it from her body, revealing her round, full breasts and puckered nipples.

She gazed at him, watching him admire her body.

"Do you like what you see?" she asked.

"You have no idea." His cock twitched in his boxers, begging to be released.

"I want you to touch me, Mason. And I want to touch you." The level of need in her voice made his cock painfully hard.

He cupped one soft breast and caressed. It filled his hand, the hard, swollen nipple pressing into his palm. He eased her back against the cushions on the side of the couch. As she leaned against them, her bright eyes watched him. He stroked her other breast, then leaned down and covered her nipple with his mouth.

"Oh, yes."

Her soft, breathy voice filled him with need. He suckled gently and she moaned. He licked her hard nub, then suckled some more. Her whimpers increased, setting his blood on fire.

His hand glided down her stomach until he found the lace of her panties. He stroked over the thin fabric, wondering if she was wet. He was rewarded with the feel of dampness that soaked right through the lace.

He had to hold himself back from gliding underneath to feel her silken folds. She arched against his hand in silent invitation.

He switched to the other nipple and lapped at it with his tongue, then sucked softly.

"Oh, Mason, I need you so much. Please, when—"

But he covered her lips with a finger, stopping her words.

"We don't want to rush this," he answered.

She laughed breathily. "I don't think ten years is rushing."

He laughed. "Well, that may be true, but what's important is tonight, and the culmination of our long journey of obsession and desire."

"Obsession?"

He leaned close to her ear and murmured, "Well, we both must be pretty obsessed to still feel this strongly after all this time." He brushed his lips against the side of her neck, loving her little gasp of delight. "And you. You actually kept your virginity for me." He said it teasingly, but she dropped her gaze to his chest.

Was it true? Had she really turned down other men in hopes that one day she might do with him what they were about to do?

True or not, he was making her uncomfortable and that would make her tense.

He stroked her shoulders. "I was teasing, Dana."

Then he stroked her breasts and cupped them in his hands. She smiled and her eyelids fell closed. She mewed softly as he lavished attention on her soft mounds. Caressing them. Licking her nipples, then suckling softly.

"I want to touch you, Mason."

He smiled and stood up, then peeled away his boxers. She watched him with wide eyes, then when he stood in front of her, she gently wrapped her hand around him, her fingers not quite reaching all the way around his thick shaft. She began gliding up and down.

Now it was his turn to moan. Her touch set him on fire. His eyelids fell closed at her gentle strokes, then popped back open when he felt her lips cover his cockhead. She had it fully in her mouth before he could protest.

He ran his fingers through her hair as she slid further down his shaft, and he eased her head back.

"Dana, that's not a good idea. I'm already well past ready."

She smiled, then licked his tip, sending quivers through him.

"But you are so full of restraint. I think you can handle it." Then she glided on him and took him deep, and sucked.

The intense sensations, paired with his need to control her, sent anger flaring through him.

She should do as she was told. He would never put up with this from his subs.

He tightened his hold on her hair and coiled it around his hand, ready to pull her away, but she squeezed him in her mouth and he couldn't do it. It felt too warm and exquisitely pleasurable being right there. Filling her mouth and throat.

She glided back, then slid deep again. He groaned.

Her hands found his balls and she caressed them, her soft, feminine touch stirring him more than he could fathom. His groin ached with the need to thrust into her. To fill her throat again and again until he found sweet release by pumping his load into her.

She squeezed him in her mouth and pleasure swelled in him.

Fuck, he was too damn close!

Frustration lurched through him at the fact she wasn't obeying him. He was used to a woman doing exactly what he told her.

His cock twitched and he tugged on her hair, still wound around his hand, pulling her head from his quivering member. She sucked in a breath and her gaze shot to his, her eyes wide in alarm.

"Dana, I told you we needed to go slow," he said through gritted teeth. But the need in him was intensifying and he felt his control unraveling.

His gaze glided down her body, falling on her skimpy panties. He tucked his fingers under the elastic and drew them down. She lay down and raised her hips so he could pull them lower, then he slid them down her legs and dropped them to the floor.

He dipped his finger between her damp folds. The feel of her hot, slick flesh drove his desire to the limit. She opened her legs and he slid his finger inside, keeping a tight rein on himself, allowing only a fingertip. Then slowly pushing in deeper, watching her face for any sign of distress.

Instead, her blue eyes were filled with desire.

He slid a second finger inside, and pushed in a little
deeper. Then she arched, pushing his fingers deeper still. He
groaned and pushed all the way, then stroked her velvety,
untouched opening. Slowly, he slid in a third finger, stretching her tight passage, preparing her for his cock.

But her opening was so narrow . . .

"Oh, Mason, that feels so good."

He started to draw his fingers out, plagued with second
thoughts, but she grabbed his wrist, stopping him.

"Mason?"

"Dana, I'm sorry, I don't think this is a good idea."

She gazed at him with wide doe eyes and murmured,
"You can't stop now. Please, you promised."

Anger flared through him. Why was she pushing him?
He did everything he could to ensure he didn't do anything
she didn't want him to, yet she seemed to care nothing for
what he wanted.

And right now, he wanted to stop this.

He wrenched his wrist from her grip, pulling his fingers from her passage. But as soon as he was free, he felt an
agony of need, wanting to feel her velvet heat around him
again.

She lay there, her legs wide, her enchanting pussy open
to him.

Dana was desperate. She needed Mason so badly, she would
do anything to entice him. She reached for his cock and
stroked it. She opened her legs wider, then arched her
body.

"Please, Mason. Fill me with your big cock."

And it was big. Swelling in her hand as he watched her, his midnight blue eyes filled with emotion and intense desire.

He leaned into her hand and, encouraged, she stroked him faster. His engorged member pulsed in her hand, as if it would burst at any moment. She drew it closer to her and he knelt between her knees.

Oh, yes, she needed to feel him inside her. She pressed him to her needy flesh and glided him along her folds. He groaned.

A battle seemed to be waging in his eyes, and she sensed he was losing his control.

She stroked him again and pressed him against her opening, readying herself for his slow, steady penetration.

"I need you, Mason. Please fill me."

As if acting on her words without thought, he drove forward. She gasped at the feel of his thick cock driving deep into her yielding flesh. Pain seared through her as he thrust deep into her, his body covering hers, pinning her to the bed.

Then his whole body stiffened, his arms holding the bulk of his weight, and she realized he was trembling.

"Fuck," he muttered, his voice tight and angry.

He drew his head up and gazed at her. She realized her body was quivering, too, at the shock of his invasion.

"Dana, I . . ." Then he turned his head away. "God damn it."

He started to pull away, but she wrapped her arms around his waist and held tight.

He stopped resisting and silence hung between them. The pain had diminished and she was getting used to the feel of his big, thick cock inside her.

"Dana, I'm so sorry. There's nothing I can ever do that will make up for this."

"Sure there is." She smiled. "Finish the job."

He frowned. "You're taking this too lightly. This was your first time and I . . ." His eyes flared with anger, and she realized it was at himself. "I fucking drove into you like a barbarian."

She stroked up his back and over his shoulder.

"Mason, you're taking this too seriously."

"But your first time should be tender and loving. It should be special."

She smiled. "It is." She nuzzled his neck. "It's with you."

"But I—"

She covered his lips with her finger. "You lost control. Because you wanted me so much. How could I not love that?"

His expression softened, the anger and frustration seeping away. He pressed his forehead to hers. "Dana, you're too forgiving."

She wiggled beneath him, shifting his cock inside her, sending wonderful, thrilling sensations through her.

"That may be true"—she laughed—"but I might not forgive you if you don't start moving soon." She grinned.

"I mean, from what I understand, there's more to it than this, right?"

Anger burned through Mason at his own incredible self-ishness and lack of control. He'd driven into her, causing her obvious pain. He'd betrayed her total trust in him.

He'd been a fucking idiot.

And yet, here she was, her face beaming with a radiant smile, her enchanting beauty mesmerizing.

She gazed at him, her luminous blue eyes filled with desire. Wanting him to make love to her. And the feel of her around him, her tight passage embracing his aching erection, was too much to resist.

"Yes, my love, there is definitely more." He brushed his lips over hers in a gentle kiss, then deepened it.

She slid her arms up his back and around his neck, her mouth moving under his.

Their mouths parted and he captured her gaze. He watched her as he slowly, and oh so gently, drew back, gliding his cock along her passage. Her eyes widened a little, but he saw no distress.

When he was almost all the way out, he kissed her softly. "Are you ready?"

She nodded, but seemed a little tense.

"This time, I'll take it slow. Okay?"

She nodded again and he felt her relax a little.

Painfully slowly, he eased forward, his cockhead pushing into her tight opening.

It was blissful, feeling her gripping him intimately as he moved deeper into her. It took everything he had not to thrust forward, driven by the intense yearning to feel her embracing his full length again. Being all the way inside her was like finding his way home. The only place in the world where he fully belonged. He fought back a huge well of emotion that could easily bring him to tears.

Her lovely eyes glowed softly as he filled her ever deeper, moving slowly, tempering his insistent need to thrust forward and claim her with his desire to guide her to exquisite pleasure.

This was for her. His cherished Dana.

"Oh, Mason," she murmured, her voice filled with joyful desire.

She needed him inside her.

She wanted him.

His cock continued forward, almost all the way in. Then she squeezed him inside and he groaned, jolting in the last inch. She moaned, her eyes wide and glowing.

His heart sang at being here again. So deep inside her. He felt himself tremble against her, his pulse pounding in his ears.

She clung to his shoulders. "You feel so good inside me." She squeezed again, sending his cock twitching.

"If you keep doing that, I'm going to lose it again and things will pick up faster than you might like."

She smiled and kissed under his chin. "Bring it on."

God, she was fearless. She was new at this, but willing to dive right in.

But it was up to him to stay grounded and ensure she enjoyed this to the fullest.

He kissed her. "We need to keep it slow for now."

She gripped his shoulders and arched up beneath him. "I love how it feels when you glide into me slowly, but now I want to feel it faster. I want to feel you moving inside me, and . . . I don't know. Just . . . more."

"Baby, part of this whole thing is building to the peak." He swirled his pelvis a little, eliciting a small gasp from her. "Do you trust me?"

Fuck, what was he thinking asking her that? He cursed himself, knowing he had already betrayed her faith in him, but she simply nodded, her blue eyes open and filled with trust.

"Okay." He drew back, slowly, the ridge of his cockhead dragging along her sensitive flesh.

She quivered beneath him. When he was at the limit, his shaft missing her warmth, he changed direction and glided into her again. Still slowly, but less so than last time.

"Ohhhhhhh," she murmured as he filled her, driving up his desperation to be home again, fully inside her.

Her fingers clutched his shoulders, her nails digging into his flesh, setting a fire inside him.

When he drew back this time, it was faster than he intended, and even faster when he glided into her. She gasped as he penetrated fully this time.

"Are you okay?" he asked in concern.

"Oh, God, yes." Her nails dragged along the skin of his back. "Please . . . I need more."

Her words, and the rapt glow in her eyes, drove him over the edge. He drew back, then glided deep. She gasped at his invasion, but clearly in pleasure. His body took over and his pelvis rocked in a steady, gentle motion. Pulling out, driving deep.

"Mason, yes." Her soft moan filled him with sudden need.

He'd been ignoring the pleasure building in his own body, shutting it out so he could concentrate on her, but her soft murmurs and the sensual rhythm of her body caressing his cock filled him with bliss.

Like a man possessed, his movements sped up until he was thrusting into her. She moaned, her nails biting into him now, driving him wild. He drove deeper and faster. She squeezed him as he entered her and he groaned.

He stroked her hair from her face. "Baby, I'm close."

He bit back his question about whether she was close. This was new to her. It was one thing to bring her to climax with his tongue or his fingers like he'd already done. That was focused. Easier to ensure her pleasure. But many women found it difficult to climax with penetration alone. Maybe she—

She arched against him and gasped, then let loose a long, erratic moan. He gazed at her face, as he continued to ride her, seeing the bliss glowing from her eyes. He drove faster, feeling his groin tightening, and filling with heat. She gasped as he drove deep, then moaned even louder.

It was too much. His cock swelled and he exploded. Not just erupting into her sweet warmth, but blasting into a new dimension of time and space . . . infinite . . . yet fully contained in this one moment . . . in this one place . . . with Dana and him sharing this bliss as if one being. Joy burst through him as he reached the pinnacle, feeling utterly and wholly complete . . . for the first time in his life.

Dana clung to Mason, his big, hard cock still deep inside her.

That had been incredible. His thick shaft gliding into her. Driving her pleasure higher and higher, until she'd burst into ecstasy.

She was glad she had waited. Held off on giving herself to a man so that this had been possible. Being with Mason was all she'd ever dreamed of, and now that she'd lived the dream, she was overjoyed. It had been everything she'd hoped for.

He shifted, then drew back, his cock slipping from her. As he settled on the bed beside her, she immediately missed his big body on top of her, and the feel of him inside her.

She gazed at him, his head on the pillow next to hers. Should she talk? Should she just curl up against him?

Or did he need space now?

She didn't know what was expected. What she should do.

But she was being silly. This was Mason.

She stroked his chest. "Thank you, Mason."

He glanced at her, and the sight of his eyes dark and full of emotion startled her.

"Is something wrong?" she asked.

"No, of course not."

But she wasn't so sure.

She drew her hand away, but he grasped it before it could escape, then pressed her palm to his mouth. The feel of his lips pressed against her flesh sent her heart skittering.

"Dana. Thank *you*."

Joy swelled through her at the warmth in his voice, but the somber look in his deep blue eyes unsettled her. She rolled toward him and swept an errant hair from his forehead, then smiled. A raft of emotions swirled in his eyes, but he reached for her and drew her against him, his hand cupping her head and pulling it to his heart. The steady beat soothed her.

He tugged the rumpled sheets from under them and drew them over their bodies.

She felt herself reluctantly dozing off, wanting to linger in the joyful afterglow of their sublime encounter. Her eyelids dropped closed.

Mason held Dana close, her breathing deepening as she drifted into sleep.

God, she had given him such a tender gift and he had been a total oaf. He pressed his lips to her hair and kissed it softly. She was everything to him and he wanted her so badly. He longed to roll her over right now and take her all over again.

But she needed sleep and he . . . Damn it, he needed to think.

He would love nothing better than to bring her into his life completely. To marry her and keep her by his side always. But that wouldn't work. Even beyond the total calamity of everything that would be thrown at them, from their families, from friends, from everyone around them, he couldn't do it.

He was wrong for her.

He could tell that she hoped this relationship would continue after the two weeks they'd agreed to. That once he'd tasted what it would be like to be with her, he wouldn't want it to end.

And that was exactly what had happened.

But it would end. It had to.

He didn't want to break her heart, so he would talk to her. Be gentle. Explain exactly why they couldn't be together, so she wouldn't feel rejected. She was an intelligent young woman. She might not like it, but she would understand.

She was fully asleep now, so he slipped from the bed without disturbing her. He needed a little space right now. He grabbed his boxers and pulled them on, then glanced back at her as he started toward the couch.

And stopped cold.

The white sheets were marred by a dark stain. Bloodred.

He sucked in a breath.

That stain represented what he'd stolen from her. Her sweet, gentle innocence had been violently torn away. By him. And worse, he wouldn't even stay by her side for the long run, even though she clearly believed she was in love with him.

He would abandon her. At least, emotionally.

That's how she'd see it, anyway. Him walking away from the love she offered.

But he knew that doing otherwise would cause her greater pain.

Dana awoke to find Mason standing at the foot of the bed watching her. She smiled, but her smile faded at his grim expression.

"We need to talk," he said.

Her stomach clenched. Talk? That sounded ominous.

Her heart sank. Was this it? Was he going to send her away now? But he'd promised two weeks.

"Are you mad at me, Mason?"

"Mad? No, of course not." He moved to the side of the bed and sat down beside her.

As her gaze flickered over the sheets, it caught on a stain marring the white linen.

Blood.

Her cheeks heated. His gaze followed hers.

He hadn't wanted to take her virginity. He'd just wanted to give her the money, but she had insisted on this. Forcing him to follow through on her contract. He'd made love to her only to ensure she took the money.

He cared about her, but not in the way she wanted. And now that the deed was done, clearly he was ending their time together.

She dragged her gaze from the bloody stain to his face. He was watching her intently.

"I . . ." But unwanted emotion welled in her, closing her throat. She sucked in a breath, then felt the tears pushing at her eyes. She scurried to the opposite side of the bed, tugging the sheet with her, then bundled it around her as she raced for the bathroom.

Mason cursed himself as he stared at the closed bathroom door. He waited, knowing she needed some time, but when she hadn't come out after fifteen minutes, he couldn't handle it any longer. He had to talk to her. Make sure she was okay.

He unlocked the door and pushed it open, then glanced inside. Dana sat on the floor, the big white sheet flowing around her fragile-looking body in a crumpled mass. The sight of her head hung forward, resting on her hands, tears dripping from her eyes, and the sound of her soft muffled sobs tore at his heart.

"Dana, what's wrong?" But he knew what was wrong.

He sucked in a breath. "You regret what we've done," he said.

She'd said she wanted this, but he'd known it was a bad idea. He should have protected her. From herself as well as from his urges.

"Dana?" He knelt down beside her, resting his hand on her arm, needing to touch her again.

She peered up at him, her eyes puffy and red. "No, Mason. I don't regret it."

She reached for his hand and took it in hers, then rested her cheek against the back of it. The sweetness of her soft touch gripped his very soul with need.

"I'll never regret it." Her eyes shimmered with tears again, and she shook her head.

He sat down on the cold tile floor beside her. "Then tell me what's wrong."

She shrugged, wiping her eyes on the sheet.

"I knew this wasn't going to last. That it couldn't last." She shrugged again. "I didn't really think it through . . . how I would feel . . . Not that I would have changed anything. But now . . . When you said we have to talk." She shook her head. "Well, that's never good. That always means something is going to end. So you aren't even going to give me until the end of our two weeks."

He compressed his lips. What could he say?

She just nodded and leaned against him, resting her head against his shoulder. He slid his arm around her and she snuggled in closer, her head now resting on his chest.

Her breathing evened out. Uttering her concern, and taking his silence as confirmation, seemed to have calmed her. Allowing her to move on to acceptance.

Her breath wisped across his chest and, despite his need to comfort her, his body heated at her physical closeness. Knowing she was naked beneath the sheet loosely wrapped around her, his groin tightened.

Then he heard a soft giggle. He glanced down at the top of Dana's head.

"What is it?" he asked.

She tipped her head and gazed up at him, amusement glittering in her eyes. "Well, here we are in this emotionally charged moment, sitting on the cold floor in a bathroom, and your . . . uh . . ." She glanced down his body again. "Your thing is standing at attention, ready for action."

He chuckled. "My thing?"

She met his gaze again, light dancing in her eyes. "Yeah, your thing."

"You had no trouble identifying it earlier. I think you called it . . . Now what was it again? Penis?" He shook his head. "No, that wasn't it. Dick? Or . . ."

She grinned. "Erection?"

"No, that wasn't it. I think maybe the word you used was 'cock.' "

She shook her head. "Oh, no. I don't think I'd use that word." Then she grinned impishly as she turned in his arms, her body resting across his chest. "There is one word I know I would call it, though."

"And what would that be?" he asked.

She leaned in and brushed her lips against his neck, sending ripples of awareness through him, right to his growing cock. Then he felt her warm, soft fingers wrap around him, and his breath caught.

"Magnificent," she answered.

She stroked him, stoking his need. He wrapped his arms around her and stood up, lifting her to her feet. His mouth found hers and her tongue glided into his mouth, her hand still wrapped around him. He twitched within her grip. His hand slid to her ass and he pulled her in tight, rocking his pelvis toward her.

Her hand slipped from him as she eased back a little and opened the sheet. It dropped to the floor and she pressed her naked body close to his again. The heaven of feeling her soft, round breasts cushioned against him set his heart beating faster.

He wanted her again. Desperately.

But the blood on the discarded white sheet lying on the tiled floor reminded him of her state.

"The shower," he murmured against her ear, then turned her and guided her to the glass door.

He drew her into the big, tiled shower with him and pressed her to the wall, kissing her as he turned on the water. Once it was the right temperature, he guided her under the flow. She kissed him, her hands stroking downward until she found his erection again, but he gripped her shoulders and turned her away from him to face the spray of water. Then he wrapped his arms around her waist and drew her close.

Dana rested back against Mason, loving the size and strength of his big body behind her. So comforting. He grabbed a bar of soap from the holder in the wall and glided it over her stomach. Round and round. Then he took the bar in his hands and soaped them up, discarded it, and glided his hands over her breasts. The feel of his slick, sudsy hands gliding over them again and again filled her with heated need.

Then his soapy hands glided down her stomach, then lower. They slid between her legs and stroked over her intimate folds. But not the light touch of a lover during foreplay. Instead, his hands glided over her in steady, sure strokes, massaging her flesh over and over again. His confident strokes almost seemed disinterested, except that she could feel his hard, swollen cock pressed against her back.

"Oh, Mason, I want you inside me."

He nuzzled her ear, then murmured, "You want what inside you?"

She giggled. "I want your cock inside me."

One of his hands slid away from her, then she felt him grip his cock and the hot, hard flesh press against her. The large, bulbous head pushed against her yielding softness, then eased inside. She was still sore from their first time, but the small amount of pain was not enough to deter her growing hunger for him.

His big head stretched her wide. Pushing deeper. Until that thickest part of him was all the way inside her.

He continued pushing into her slowly. Oh, so slowly she thought she'd die of need.

"Mason," she murmured, overwhelmed by the intensity of joining with him.

His lips brushed her neck in light kisses as his cock pushed deeper still. The thickness of him stretching her. Filling her further than she thought possible.

His arm came around her body again, his hand flattening on her stomach. His other hand still rested on the front of her mound.

She drew in some air, resting her head back against his solid chest.

"You feel so good inside me."

He kissed her ear, then rocked his pelvis back, dragging his cockhead along her inner passage, then forward, pushing deep again.

"Oh, yes," she murmured on a sigh.

"And you feel so good around me." He rocked again, and she squeezed him inside. His groan stoked the fire inside her.

He continued to rock his pelvis, gliding within her. Sending electricity crackling through her.

He started pumping deeper, his body rocking against her, his big cock caressing her deeply. She began to tremble as her body blazed with desire and need. Pleasure rising inside her.

He thrust deeply into her now, his hands holding her tight to his body. His fingers found her clit and his first incendiary touch sparked joy within her. When his fingers glided over the bundle of nerves, her eyes widened at the intensity, then she moaned softly. The feel of the shower raining on her skin and his fingers coaxing her pleasure higher was simply exquisite.

She cried out as joy burst through her, carrying her higher and higher until all conscious thought fled. Ecstasy filled her as she moaned long and loud, the sound echoing around them in the tiled space.

He continued gliding into her as she rode the wave of pleasure, then he slowed, holding her tightly against him. His lips played along her neck as they stood, enmeshed together, his big cock still hard and twitching inside her.

Finally, he drew back, slipping himself from her body, and turned her.

"Mason, but you haven't—"

He smiled down at her. "We're not finished yet."

He pressed her back against the tile wall and she felt his big cock slide into her again, entering her easily this time. His pelvis ground against her as his cock filled her completely.

The heat in his eyes as he gazed at her was intense. She could almost believe . . .

She reached up and stroked his cheek, their gazes locked.

"Mason, I—"

But he started to move, his cock stroking her inner passage as he drew back. Then he slowly glided forward again. His hot, hard flesh caressed her with each stroke. Slow and smooth. Pleasure fluttered through her like hot silk on a summer breeze. Calm and pleasant.

His sure strokes made her melt. The glow of her recent orgasm blazed brighter and she could feel the heat building once again.

She drew in a breath as she realized that . . . oh, God, it could be this easy. Pleasure effortlessly building. Filling her with each smooth, steady stroke of his cock. Until the heat washed over her and . . .

She clung to his shoulders. "Oh, Mason, I'm . . ." She moaned.

"Yes, sweetheart." He gazed at her, his eyes glowing with incandescent heat. "Come for me."

His words were too much. She gasped, then moaned as ecstasy swelled through her again in steady, cresting waves of sheer joy.

His thrusts sped up, his smooth strokes carrying her higher and higher. Her body shook within his arms as he drove into her faster and faster.

"Oh, God, Dana." He surged deep, pressing her tight to the shower wall, then flooded her insides with liquid heat.

He groaned at his release and she squeezed him inside her. Then he slumped forward.

She wrapped her arms around him, loving his warm body so close to hers.

He drew back, smiling down at her.

"Oh, Mason . . ." Feelings welled up inside her and she couldn't stop herself from uttering the words that fluttered in her heart. "I love you."

Mason's heart nearly stopped at her words, and her eyes widened as soon as she realized what she'd just said.

He tried to hide the maelstrom of emotions her words elicited, but his clenched jaw and stony expression gave him away. Watching her cringe, pain flashing through her eyes, made his gut clench.

"Mason, I'm sorry. I didn't mean to—"

He took her mouth fiercely, stopping her words. Pulling her tight to him. Not wanting her to hurt, but knowing he could not reciprocate her words.

It could *never* work between them.

No matter how much he wanted it to.

When he pulled his mouth away, his expression still filled with anguish, he turned off the shower, then took her arm and guided her to the glass door. Before they stepped out, though, his gaze caught on a dot of deep red marring the pristine white tile floor of the shower. Then another.

He stepped back and his gaze glided up Dana's legs. Another drop fell. Then he noticed a couple of red droplets on her inner thigh.

Blood.

"Dana, what the hell?"

She glanced downward. "Oh, they said this might happen."

"Who is they?" he demanded.

Her gaze lifted to his. "I . . . uh . . . did some research about losing my virginity and some of the articles said that there might be blood for a few hours afterward." She bit her lip. "Just a little."

He just stared at the crimson droplets, swirling with the water. Spreading.

"Does it hurt?" he asked.

Her teeth worked at her lower lip. "No." But as he continued to pin her with an unflinching stare, she sighed. "A little. But it's no big deal."

"What did these articles say about that?"

"Just that it's different for everyone, but some women do feel pain for a while after. They suggested taking over-the-counter painkillers, but I don't usually bother—"

He took her hand, pushed open the shower door, and led her to the medicine cabinet, then grabbed a bottle of painkillers. He spilled out two caplets and handed them to her, then filled a paper cup from the dispenser with water.

"Take them."

She gazed up at him and hesitated, then popped the pills in her mouth and swallowed some water.

"What else can I do for you?" he asked.

"I need a feminine napkin. There's some in my purse."

He nodded. "Stay here."

He quickly dried off and wrapped the towel around

his waist, then strode out of the bathroom and across the suite to where her pink sequined evening bag was lying on the floor by the couch. He picked it up, then glanced around for her underwear. The scrap of pink lace was lying on the floor by the bed. She probably needed something more substantial than that. He went to Dana's room, punched in the combination, and opened the door.

When he stepped inside, he felt surrounded by her. There were traces of her everywhere. Her sweetness and her femininity were evident in the frilly cushions, the brush and mirror set on her dresser, the delicate figurines of fairies and angels on the bookshelf. Those ornaments she had left behind when his father and her mother had divorced, as if she'd wanted to leave behind all the memories of being here. But she'd taken her books. He remembered the wide range she used to have on these shelves. An eclectic selection of novels, biographies, history texts, and several other disciplines had clearly shown her intellectual acumen, even at only eighteen.

He walked to the dresser and pulled open drawers until he found one full of underwear. It was a colorful, lacy jumble. He picked up a pair of fuchsia panties, then purple, but both were skimpy and . . . sexy. He swept through the mass of lace and satin until he spied a white pair. He snatched them up. Simple. Cotton. Substantial looking.

He wrapped his hand around them and returned to the bathroom in his suite. He knocked.

"Come in," Dana called.

He stepped inside to find her sitting on the small bench, a big, white towel wrapped around her. He handed her the panties and her purse. She looked at the white garment, then frowned.

"Really? Granny panties?"

"I thought they'd work better . . . you know. With the thing."

She laughed. "Men. You get so squeamish around feminine products." She unzipped her purse and fumbled inside, then pulled out a small, pink package.

"I'll be in the bedroom," he said.

"Okay."

He grabbed the soiled bedsheet and left the room, closing the door behind him. He retrieved some fresh sheets from the linen closet, and was just finishing making the bed when Dana came out of the bathroom. He tossed the heap of old sheets in the corner and turned toward her.

Her arms were crossed over her breasts, and all she wore were the panties he'd brought her. The sight of her in those plain white panties, hugging her hips and rising to an inch below her navel, was oddly sexy. So innocent. So . . . virginal.

A spike thrust through his heart.

What kind of idiot had he been to take her virginity? He'd hurt her . . . caused her to bleed. And, fuck, knowing how she felt about him, it was inevitable that she would believe it could lead to more. The emotional pain would be far more scarring than the physical.

"Let's get some sleep, baby."

He took her elbow and drew her into his arms. She wrapped her arms around him as he held her close, loving the feel of her soft, naked breasts cushioned against him.

He nuzzled her ear, then guided her to the bed. She climbed under the covers as he turned out the light, then he slid in beside her. She snuggled back against him and he wrapped his arms around her, then cupped one round breast in his hand.

"Good night," he murmured.

Mason could feel Sylvie next to him in the darkness. Warm and soft against him.

But Sylvie knew better than to climb into his bed without permission. She slept on the couch in his room, waiting to serve at his pleasure. If she'd come into his bed, it was to entice him to punish her.

"Roll over," he demanded.

The shadowy shape beside him rolled over. He slid his arm under her stomach and lifted her lower torso, then slid a pillow under her, raising her ass. He raised his hand and slapped her ass. She cried out. He slapped again.

"You aren't allowed in my bed unless I invite you."

"But—"

He smacked again, the cracking sound ringing through the room.

"I'm going to punish you and you will stay silent."

He grabbed her long, dark hair and coiled it around his hand, then pulled it tight, drawing her head back from the pillow.

He leaned close to her ear. "Understand?"

She nodded.

"Good."

He smacked her bottom again. Then again.

Sylvie liked to be slapped.

He stroked his hand over her round ass, then tugged her head up again and nibbled her earlobe.

"Do you want me to spank you harder?" He only asked to build her excitement. Sylvie always wanted him to spank her harder.

"No."

Her plaintive tone caught him off guard.

"What the hell, Sylvie?"

"Who's Sylvie?"

She was just a shadowy shape beside him but he didn't have to see her face to realize . . . it was Dana's voice.

He sucked in a breath, then rolled onto his back.

"Shit."

When he'd woken up to her soft body next to his, he'd thought she was Sylvie. He'd *wanted* her to be Sylvie, desperately needing to be a Dom again.

He loved the tenderness that he and Dana had shared, but he knew he needed more.

"No one important," he answered. "Just someone I know casually."

Dana tugged the pillow from beneath her stomach and dropped it on the floor, then rolled toward him.

"You seemed to be having a not-so-casual dream about her just now."

"I'm sorry, Dana. I was asleep. It didn't mean anything."

"But why are you dreaming about her when you're here with me?"

He could hear the hurt in her voice. How could he make her understand that it was just that he had needs she couldn't meet for him?

He'd had a life before the two of them started this whole thing, and he would have a life after they parted at the end of their two weeks. Maybe it would be better not to say anything. She had to get used to the fact she was only in his bed for a short time.

"This Sylvie . . . you treat her differently in bed than you do me."

"That's true. She meets a different need for me."

"What kind of need?"

Fuck, did she really want to get into this now?

"Dana, I don't really want to start this conversation in the middle of the night."

"But I want to know. She meets different needs for you. If I understood them better, maybe I could—"

"No."

"But—"

"I said no, Dana."

"Mason, I—"

He rolled onto her, holding his weight on his arms, her trapped between them, and glared down at her. "This stubbornness of yours is exactly why you can't meet those needs. Now go to sleep or I'll send you to your room."

She frowned but held her silence.

He rolled onto his side again, then wrapped his arms around her waist and pulled her into a spooning position, facing away from him.

"Now go to sleep."

Dana lay in Mason's arms and sighed. She had been an idiot for telling him she loved him in the shower. But the words had just slipped out.

She knew Mason wouldn't allow this relationship to continue. She'd always known it. But she was a dreamer and in all her dreams, she wound up in a happily-ever-after relationship with Mason. Spending her life with him, as husband and wife.

That was her biggest and brightest dream. She'd give up almost anything for it.

But her blurting out an "I love you" just made things worse. That's probably why he'd dreamed of another woman. One who didn't stress him out with unwanted emotions.

One he could allow himself to fall in love with because she wasn't his stepsister.

The way he'd handled her when he'd thought she was Sylvie was . . . disturbing. And exhilarating. He'd punished her, smacking her bottom until it burned. But it had excited her. And when he'd tugged on her hair, pulling her head back . . . shivers had quivered through her.

Dana picked up the tray that held orange juice in a crystal glass, a fine china coffee cup filled with steaming coffee, a china plate with a silver cover to keep the contents warm, silverware, and a pristine white linen napkin. She carried it to the dresser and set it down, then turned to the bed.

Mason lay there with his arm casually thrown over his face, the blankets sprawled across his waist, baring his broad muscular chest and shoulders. She wanted to climb right back into bed with him. To reach under the covers and find out if he was hard, then stroke him awake.

But she was haunted by what had happened last night.

Mason had taken her virginity and then only hours later had dreamt about another woman. And then, when she'd questioned him, he'd told her she didn't meet his needs.

Her heart ached.

He met *her* needs. Every one of them.

Except for loving her back, of course. And that tore at her soul.

As if Mason could feel her scrutiny, he opened his eyes. He blinked, then gazed in her direction.

"Good morning," he murmured, his voice sleep-roughened.

She longed to sit on the bed beside him and stroke his raspy, whisker-shadowed jaw. To press her lips to his chin and drag her teeth along the coarse stubble, then run her hands down his sculpted chest.

"Good morning," she responded. "I have breakfast for you."

She turned and lifted the tray, then carried it to the bed.

He pushed himself upright and she set the tray on his lap. She lifted the silver top from the plate.

"Eggs and bacon and those silver dollar pancakes you used to love so much."

He smiled and gazed up at her. "You made this?"

Her cheeks heated. "No, I asked the butler to arrange it. I would have, but you didn't have the ingredients in the kitchenette."

"It's okay, Dana. You don't have to cook for me. I was just curious."

She sat on the chair near the bed. "I would like to cook for you."

He laughed as he poured syrup from a tiny silver pitcher onto his pancakes. "Okay, we'll arrange that sometime." He glanced at her. "Have you already eaten?"

"No, my breakfast is on the table."

"Get it and we'll eat together."

She nodded absently as she watched him take a bite of one of the small pancakes.

"Mason?"

He tilted his head toward her, then frowned at her serious expression. "What is it, Dana?"

"The conversation we started last night . . . When you said I didn't meet your needs . . ."

He put down his fork, his expression grim, hesitating.

The silence was too much for her, so she had to fill it. "When you were dreaming about that other woman . . . Sylvie . . . the way you made love to her . . ." It reminded her of when she'd seen him with the maid. "I think I should tell you that I once saw you and . . ." She sucked in a breath. "I saw you and Maria . . . uh . . . having sex in the den."

His expression turned pained. "When?" he asked sharply.

She stared at her hands, her fingers twisting around each other. "It was on prom night."

The fact that he asked her when . . . did that mean it had happened more than once? But, of course, it had. Why would she believe otherwise?

"You couldn't have seen. You'd already left with your date."

She shook her head. "I changed my mind while we were driving away. I didn't want to be with *him* that evening. I wanted to be with you. So I told him I felt sick and had him bring me back to the house, then I raced inside looking for you."

"And you found me." He frowned. "Damn it, Dana. You should never have seen that."

"I didn't really understand at the time. You seemed to be . . . forcing her." She shook her head. "But everything I knew about you told me you wouldn't do something like that."

"Fuck, Dana, I wish you hadn't . . ." His hands clenched into fists. "You shouldn't have seen that," he repeated in a low mutter. "Maria . . . she liked it rough. She liked a man to take control, and she liked to struggle. Fuck, it must have looked to you like I was raping the woman."

"I would never believe that. And even though I was still young, and inexperienced, I could tell she was . . . enjoying it." She shook her head. "But it was confusing to me."

"Dana, I'm sorry you witnessed that. But what happened after you saw us? Did you go out to your prom after all?"

She shook her head. "I went up to my room and just stayed there until morning." Sobbing her heart out.

Mason pursed his lips and nodded, probably figuring out the latter part.

"You know I struggled with my attraction to you back then," he admitted. "Being with Maria gave me a way to alleviate that yearning."

So it wasn't just the one time.

Dana's heart sank at the thought that he could so easily escape his desire for her, which meant it had only been a physical attraction, nothing more.

He lifted the tray from his lap and set it on the bed beside him, then sat on the side of the bed.

"Dana, I think it's time we had a little talk."

"About why you said I don't meet your needs?"

"That's right."

A low trilling sound caught his attention and he picked up his cell phone from the bedside table and glanced at it. His lips tightened and he glanced at Dana again.

"It seems this conversation will have to wait. I have to go meet someone."

"Now? But—"

His sharp gaze spiked through her and she fell silent.

He stood up and, totally naked, walked to the bathroom. Once the door closed, she couldn't help herself. She hurried to the bed and picked up his phone and glanced at the text he'd received.

Need to talk to you at once. It's urgent. Meet me at Le Noir right away.

It was from Maria.

Mason walked into the stodgy club, with the oak-paneled walls, elegant crystal lighting fixtures, and heavy wooden furniture. He stepped into the private room Maria had reserved for them, then closed the door behind him. Maria, dressed in an elegant, tailored jacket and matching skirt in dark blue silk, sat on a leather sofa, a decanter of white wine in front of her. She held a tall, stemmed crystal glass in her hand.

"There you are, Mason."

"Hello, Maria."

She placed her glass on the round table in front of the couch, then stood and walked toward him, smiling. "Surely I get a kiss."

He leaned in to kiss her cheek, but she turned her head and pressed her lips to his, wrapping her arms around his neck and pulling him close. As her tongue glided into his mouth, he grasped her hands and tugged them from his neck, then pressed her away from him.

"That's not really appropriate, Maria."

"Really? We used to do far more than that."

"Yes, before you became my stepmother."

She laughed. "Ah, it's inappropriate to give your step-mother a kiss, but fucking your stepsister is quite acceptable."

He frowned. "How do you know about that?"

She rested her hand on his upper arm. "Mason, we both knew it was inevitable."

He walked to the leather chair facing the couch and settled into it, not willing to play this touching game with Maria. "I asked how you knew."

She strolled back to the couch and poured him a glass of wine. She handed it to him, then sat down again.

"Still playing the maid, I see," he said.

She smiled seductively. "I'm willing to play a lot more with you. I'm sure the staff could bring me a maid's cos-tume pretty quickly and we could replay some of our finer moments."

"None of our moments were fine, Maria," Mason said grimly.

She leaned forward. "That's not true, Mason. Some of my finest moments were with you."

He almost thought her eyes looked a little misty at those words.

"And surely you are at least a little thankful at how I helped you survive your lust for your little stepsister. How would you have gotten through that time without me?" She picked up her wine and took a sip.

"Which leads us back to the question of how you know about Dana and me."

She sighed and leaned back against the couch. "Is it really so hard to guess? The dim-witted little brat put her picture up on that website, offering her innocence to the highest bidder." She raised an eyebrow at Mason. "You really didn't think about the fact that that's exactly the type of site your father would follow?"

Fuck, of course it was. His father was . . . sick. He'd always wanted his women young. *Too* young.

Mason's stomach clenched. Fuck, the apple hadn't fallen far from the tree. After all, he'd lusted after Dana himself since she was sixteen.

The difference was that Mason hadn't acted on it.

Until now.

"Fuck, Maria." So Chas knew that Dana had offered to sell her virginity. "But how did he know I was the buyer?"

Maria crossed her legs, her high-heel-clad foot rocking nervously. "When he saw her picture on there, he became obsessed." Her gaze settled on his, and he could see the anxiety in her eyes. "He was adamant about buying her contract. But when he contacted them, he found it was already sold." She waved a hand in the air. "Of course, the service wouldn't tell him to whom, but you know your father. He wouldn't take no for an answer, so he used his contacts and several bribes to find out." She sighed. "When he learned it was you who had bought her . . ." She pursed her lips. "That it was you who was going to fuck her for the first time . . . he was livid."

Her gaze sharpened. "That's why I told you it was urgent that we talk. I wanted to warn you. Your father is more than furious about this. The two of you locked horns about her in the past, and you prevented him from fucking her then. And now, when she willingly offered up her virginity to the highest bidder, you swooped in and stole her right from under his nose. He is beyond reason and has decided to do something about it."

Mason's eyebrows arched. "And what might that be?"

Maria leaned forward, and her worried expression filled him with icy apprehension.

"I don't know exactly. But he said he intends to destroy you."

Her fingers tightened around her wineglass.

"And her."

Part Three

The whole drive home, Mason stewed about what Maria had told him. He didn't respect the old man, and Chas wasn't the best in business mainly because he didn't keep a clear focus, but when he put his mind to something—like revenge—he was very focused. Very underhanded. And absolutely ruthless.

Mason knew he could survive whatever his father threw at him, even though he was sure Chas could definitely do some damage, but he worried about Dana. The old man wouldn't hesitate to tear down her good name, and Mason's, even if it cast a bad light on the family as a whole. Mason didn't want Dana to have to go through that.

He might not be able to do anything in time to stop it, though. Even if Mason threatened to destroy his father's corporation—which Chas had to know Mason would do anyway if Chas hurt Dana in any way—by now Chas had enough assets that he could take the hit and still keep his decadent lifestyle.

But what Mason worried about more was if Chas would target Dana in some other way.

Fuck, he was glad that Dana would be going off to Paris for her graduate degree. She would be away from the scandal that Chas might let loose here.

But that was months away. In the meantime, he needed to find a way to protect her.

He knocked on Dana's door and a moment later she opened it.

She curled her hand around the edge of the door. "Hi."

"Sorry I had to interrupt our conversation earlier, but it was important."

She nodded, but he could tell she was upset.

"Why don't you come back to my suite and we'll continue where we left off?"

He still couldn't bring himself to go into her room, which was crazy now that they were having sex. But being in her room reminded him too much of the young Dana. The Dana he had needed—and wanted—to protect from his father.

And now, it seemed, he needed to again.

She opened the door and followed him down the hall, then he tapped in the combination and they went inside.

"Mason, are you still seeing Maria?"

He turned to her with a frown. "We still keep in touch. Why do you ask?"

He walked to the bar and poured himself a scotch, then tossed it back.

"I looked at the text message on your phone when you were in the shower." She bit her lip. "I'm sorry, I know I shouldn't have, but I couldn't help myself. I really wanted to know what was so important that it would pull you away right then."

"I think we want to continue that conversation now," he said, refusing to be pulled into the topic of Maria.

"All right." Dana sat on the couch, her legs curled beside her.

He walked to the armchair across from her and sat down.

She locked gazes with him. "So why don't I meet your needs?"

Dana watched as Mason's face turned somber. "We're both aware of the obvious reasons we can't continue a sexual relationship. But if we really wanted to, we could weather all of those. There is one thing that stops us cold, however, and it has nothing to do with what others will think about it."

Her chest tightened. "Tell me."

He sighed deeply. "You said you saw me with Maria all those years ago." His lips compressed.

She nodded.

"Those times with Maria . . . They triggered in me certain . . . urges."

"Urges?" she parroted, not sure she really wanted to hear more.

"I enjoyed the sense of power it gave me. Of control."

"But you already owned an entire company. At

twenty-six, you controlled your own corporation . . . had an entire team of executives who did whatever you said. You controlled people's jobs. Their lives."

"It wasn't the same. This was more . . . personal."

Her stomach tightened. "You liked the idea of taking her against her will? So does that mean . . . that you'd really like to . . . ?"

His harsh blue gaze locked on hers. "To rape a woman?" He shook his head. "No, of course not. But to feel her bend to my will . . . to know she will do anything I tell her." His gaze sharpened. *"Anything."* His eyes glinted like steel, sending a quiver through her. "Or suffer the consequences."

Her breath caught. "What kind of consequences?"

"Punishment."

Her eyes widened. "Like spanking?"

He nodded but she sensed there was more he wanted to say.

"I could try that. Letting you dominate me, I mean."

"Dana, what I do with a woman is not playacting. It's very real, and it's very intense. For me and for her. It only works if it's what the woman really wants. If she needs to give herself up to me with everything she is."

She sucked in a breath, but couldn't seem to get enough air. She stepped toward him and took his hand, reveling in the feel of his strong, masculine fingers around hers.

"I want you with everything I have," she murmured softly. "And I'm willing to give you whatever you want."

His lips compressed and his eyes hardened as he drew his hand from hers.

"It's not what I want, Dana. It's what I *need*." He shook his head. "And you can't just act the submissive. It won't be real."

"But—"

"You have to understand, Dana. I do this with women who want me to dominate them."

"And punish them."

"Yes."

"Let me try," she begged, not wanting to lose him.

"It won't be what you really want. That means, in time, you'll become unhappy. Even resent doing it. And start to resent me."

"No, I would never resent you."

His eyes turned ice cold. He rested his hand on the back of her head, ever so gently, and slowly ran it down her hair.

Suddenly, his hand grasped her long tresses and he tugged her head back, bending her neck. Her eyes widened in surprise.

He leaned in close, his face so near that his lips could almost brush her cheek. His breath sent tingles dancing along her neck.

Fire flashed in his ice cold gaze as it traveled the length of her body, making her tremble. "Believe me, the things I would do to you . . ." His intense stare flicked back to hers, boring through her. "You *would* resent me. Even grow to hate me."

She shook her head. "Never."

He tightened his grip, pulling her head back further.

"You will." His granite hard gaze glittered. "And if I were your master, I would never let you get away with contradicting me. You would learn to bow to my will. To do *exactly* as you are told, the instant you're told." He leaned in close to her ear and murmured grittily, "You would give yourself over to me, body and soul."

Her heart pounded in her chest, with both trepidation and excitement at his words.

"Mason, give me a chance."

He released her with a scowl. "No."

"But—"

"Dana, go to your room."

She wanted to protest, but his uncompromising expression stopped her words cold.

She turned and walked toward the door, feeling numb inside.

Mason stared at the door. The feel of Dana's hair coiled around his hand and the sight of her head pulled back exposing her throat, her eyes wide with shock and dismay, were etched into his memory.

He scowled and strode across the room to the bar, poured another scotch and gulped it down. A warmth spread through his stomach, calming his strained nerves.

Fuck, her willingness to try even after he did his best to scare her away made him long to take this relationship the rest of the way. To make her his sub and totally control her.

Heat coiled through him at the thought, and his cock swelled.

But this was Dana. Sweet, innocent Dana.

His hands clenched at his side. Not so innocent now. Thanks to him.

He poured himself another drink and sat down. He swirled the amber liquid in the glass and watched the sparkling whirlpool, allowing his thoughts to settle.

He wanted Dana with an ache that bored through his soul. If only he could just say yes to her request. If they could give it a try and see if—

Fuck. He took a gulp of his drink. If he dominated her it would be because he wanted it, not because she would enjoy it. In fact, he was sure she would be sickened by his demands.

He frowned. But maybe he could use the situation to help protect her. His father would surely start a scandal that would embarrass and hurt Dana. Mason either wanted her very close, where he could shelter her, or very far away.

He gulped the rest of his drink, a plan forming in his mind.

Dana sat on her bed and stared out the window at the bright sunshine glistening off the backyard pool, still quivering from her encounter with Mason.

The things he'd told her had shocked her, yet hadn't been totally unexpected. She'd seen him that one time with Maria. And the way he'd handled her when he'd thought she was Sylvie . . .

But she hadn't thought about the fact that he must enjoy hurting the women. That he *needed* to do that.

When he'd told her that—and said that's what they wanted—it had thrown her off-balance. But remembering as she'd struggled against him in bed . . . remembering the intense need it had triggered in her—made her wonder . . .

She heard the *plink* of her phone, indicating a text had arrived. She pulled it from her purse and glanced at the display.

Come here. I want to talk to you.

Mason was summoning her.

Butterflies fluttered in her stomach as she stood up.

She wanted Mason with all her heart. Wanted to be in his life forever. Wanted to be in his *bed*.

She walked to her dresser and brushed her hair until it shone. Then she tugged off her T-shirt and pulled on a nice knit top that clung to her slender frame and showed off her full breasts. She examined herself in the mirror.

She wanted a chance to prove to him that she could be what he wanted.

But would he give her the opportunity?

She slipped from her door and walked to his. She unlocked it and entered his domain.

"There you are." His stone-cold blue eyes stared at her. "That was far too long. From now on, I want you to respond to me instantly. Do you understand?"

His commanding tone took her breath away. She nodded, but as his gaze sharpened on her, she replied, "Yes."

"Address me as 'sir.' "

A tingle danced through her.

"Yes, sir."

Hope swirled through her. "Does this mean you'll give me a chance?"

"Show me proper respect. Drop your gaze to the floor, and keep silent until I give you permission to speak."

She stifled the urge to protest and dropped her gaze to the cream carpet beneath her feet.

"I have a proposition for you. I want you to consider it carefully, because I will not change the terms in any way. You will take it or leave it, no negotiations."

She nodded, hope flaring inside her.

"You said you wanted me to give you a chance to try being my sub, so I'm going to do exactly that."

Excitement skittered through her and she glanced up at him. "Oh, Mason. Thank you." But at his stern frown, she dropped her gaze again. "Thank you, sir."

"You will come and stay with me full time at my penthouse for the summer. You will do whatever I tell you without question. You will follow whatever rules I set forth. If you break my rules, or do anything I decide requires disciplining, then I will punish you. Do you understand so far?"

Joy swirled through her, especially when he said she'd be staying with him for the summer, making it difficult to concentrate. Something about rules and punishment. "I . . . think so, sir."

"Dana, look at me."

She obeyed and found herself faced with his sober blue eyes.

"This is not a game. Let me keep this simple. You will do exactly as I say and follow all my rules. And if you fail to do so, I will punish you. Understood?"

"Yes, sir."

"I will have a contract drawn up and there will be no negotiations. As part of this contract, I will be giving you a large sum of money, which you will use for your education in Paris. I will also pay for a nice apartment for you to live in."

"Mason, you don't have to do that."

"I said no negotiations. That is part of the contract. Take it or leave it."

She nodded. "Okay. I mean, yes, sir." She toyed with the hem of her shirt. "And what happens at the end of the summer? To us, I mean. If I meet your needs . . ." She bit her lip. "Can we be together?"

He took a sip of his drink. "Let's not get ahead of ourselves. This contract is to give you the chance to see if you can meet my needs. I'm not going to take it easy on you because it's important that you know what it will really be like to be my sub. Since there will be no negotiating the contract terms, and I believe you will quickly come to see that this is not for you, there will be a three-day trial period where you can opt out at any time. You will, however, take the monetary compensation no matter what happens during the trial period. Whenever the contract ends, be it at the end of the summer, or during the trial, you will immediately leave for Paris. Does that sound fair?"

"Yes, sir. But I don't need you to pay me."

"I said no negotiations."

She pursed her lips and nodded. "And I don't need the trial period. I will do whatever you want me to."

His lips compressed. "We'll see."

Dana sat beside Mason in the backseat of the limo as it drove smoothly along the highway. They were nearing their exit. Mason had spent the entire three-hour drive working on his tablet, totally ignoring her.

She bit her lip and stared out the window, realizing she was being oversensitive. He'd just spent almost two weeks away with her. Now he had work to catch up on.

The limo took the exit ramp and ten minutes later, they pulled up in front of Mason's apartment building. The driver opened the door and took her hand to help her from the car. Mason took her elbow and guided her to the front door as the driver pulled their bags from the trunk. The doorman opened the door for them and Mason led her across the lobby to the elevator.

Dana glanced at him, wondering if he would break the long silence between them, but he simply pushed the button and pressed his hand to her back as the door whooshed open. Soon they were stepping off the elevator into his huge penthouse.

The blazing orange vista of the setting sun filled the space with a fiery glow.

Dana stepped out of her shoes, then shed her jacket and hung it in the closet. Mason walked to the living room bar and poured himself a drink. Dana followed him, hovering anxiously, not quite sure what to do. Mason sat down on the couch. She walked toward him, but his gaze locked on her and something about his steely eyes stopped her in her tracks. She stood there, watching him, becoming more nervous and self-conscious as his gaze simply glided over her. He swirled his drink, then took a leisurely sip.

Then he leaned forward and set his glass on the glossy, ebony coffee table in front of him.

"Take off your clothes." His words, spoken so casually, shocked her.

He'd seen her naked before, but to have him sit there, still in his business suit, telling her to strip, unsettled her.

She hesitated, and his dark blue eyes turned steely.

"I said, take off your clothes."

At the edge in his tone, her hands immediately jumped to the buttons of her shirt and she unfastened them, one at a time, intensely aware of the garment opening, revealing her body to scrutiny.

As his gaze followed her fingers downward, her skin tingled. She dropped the shirt to the ground, then unfastened her jeans and pushed them to the floor, too. She peeled away her ankle socks and tossed them aside, then stood there in her white lace bra and panties.

"Keep going."

Goose bumps flashed across her skin and she felt her cheeks flush.

"Do I have to repeat myself?" he asked in a hard tone.

"N-no, sir."

She reached behind her and unhooked the bra, then dropped the straps from her shoulders, but held the garment to her body with her arm. Her cheeks flushed hotter.

This is silly. He's seen me naked.

But not like this. Where he sat there fully clothed and watched her.

She drew in a deep breath and dropped the bra to the floor. Her nipples ached as they pushed forward, tight and hard. She tucked her fingers under the waistband of her lacy undies and guided them over her hips, then down her legs to the floor. Slowly, she stood up, intensely aware of her total nudity.

"Don't make me repeat myself again."

His gaze, cold and indifferent, traveled from her head to her toes, then back up again. Settling on her breasts . . . then moving lower.

She could feel the heat inside her. Spreading. Filling her with need.

Even though he seemed so distant and . . . almost disinterested . . . she wanted him. Needed him with a quiet desperation.

"Kneel down."

She lowered herself to her knees.

"Now bow down, pressing your face to the floor."

She leaned forward and placed her nose to the soft carpet, her hands on either side of her head.

"Lift your ass in the air."

She could tell by his voice that he'd stood up and was moving behind her. She followed his order, extremely conscious of the fact that her most intimate flesh was exposed to his view.

"Widen your legs. I want a better look at you."

She slid her knees further apart. She could feel his gaze on her as if it had physically brushed across her flesh.

"Do you like me looking at you like this?" he asked.

Her cheeks grew hotter. She didn't know what to say.

"Just be honest, Dana."

"No, sir." But as soon as she said it, she knew it was a lie. "I mean . . ." She bit her lip. "I do, but it's . . . embarrassing."

"You shouldn't be embarrassed about showing me your body, Dana. You are a beautiful woman. Every part of you is beautiful."

"Thank you, sir."

He walked past her and she heard him settling on the couch again.

"Come here, Dana."

She pushed herself from the floor and stood up. As she walked toward him, he sipped his drink. She stopped in front of him and he perused her naked body.

"Kneel in front of me."

He opened his legs and she lowered herself down, settling on her knees between his thighs.

"Undo my pants."

She reached for the button, noticing the bulge growing under the fine wool fabric. She released the button, then gripped the zipper tab between her fingertips and dragged it downward.

Oh, God, how she wanted to feel his hot, hard shaft in her hands.

She reached inside, anxious to see his massive erection. To press her lips to him and take him deep in her mouth.

But his hand clamped around her wrist, gripping her like a steel band, stopping her.

Her eyes widened.

"Do only what you're told to do. Do you understand?"

"Y-yes, sir."

He released her hand and she drew it away.

"Usually, I would punish you for something like that, but I'll let you off with a warning." His gaze locked on hers. "*This* time."

"Thank you, sir." But she remembered what it was like to be punished by him. To feel his hand on her behind. Would it be like that again? Or would he do something . . . harsher?

She knelt there, waiting for his command.

He drew his cock from his pants and her mouth went

dry at the sight of it. Long, hard, the veins along the side pulsing. She licked her lips, wanting to taste it.

He watched her as he wrapped his hand around it, then stroked.

"Are you wet, Dana?"

"What?" She dragged her gaze from his cock to his face. She could feel the slickness between her thighs. "Uh . . . yes, sir."

"Good. Now fuck me."

She bit her lip, startled by his command. She wasn't sure what to do with him sitting there, his cock pointing to the ceiling. He had always led before.

She stood up and took his hand, assuming he would follow her to the bedroom, but he didn't budge.

"I mean right here."

"Oh."

She glanced at the couch, wondering if she could get him to lie down, or if maybe he assumed she'd lie down and he'd actually take the lead.

"You seem confused." He took her hands and drew her forward until she was kneeling on the couch over him, his cock hovering so close to her slick folds. "Like this."

She sucked in a breath when he brushed his hard flesh against her. Then he took her hand and wrapped it around him.

"Now fuck me."

With his hard cock at her opening, she lowered herself slowly. His cockhead stretched her as she took him inside, then glided into her as she moved downward. Oh, God, he was so thick and hard. She kept going, taking him deeper, until finally, he was all the way inside and she was sitting on his lap.

They were face-to-face. His unsettling blue eyes locked on hers. She wanted to lean forward and brush her lips to his. To kiss him, and for him to kiss her back. With passion. And love.

But most of all, she wanted to wipe away the indifference in his eyes. To see the loving glow that she'd glimpsed so many times when they'd been at the mansion.

But now, sitting here with him inside her body, it was like gazing into the face of a stranger.

"Fuck me," he murmured, desire transforming his stone-cold tone to one of need.

She raised her body, relishing the feel of his big cockhead gliding along her passage, then lowered herself again.

His hands slid around her waist, but only lightly, not controlling her movements. She moved up and down, his cock filling her again and again.

Pleasure swelled through her.

She was surprised at how exciting it was to be in control. Even though he was the one commanding her, she set the pace. She controlled the movements. He allowed her to ride his body as she saw fit.

But after a few moments, he wrapped his hands around her waist and adjusted her pace, taking back control. His jaw tensed as he guided her to move faster, his big cock pulsing inside her. Thrusting deeper and harder. The sensations pounding through her were exhilarating. Pleasure built inside her, and she moaned.

He arched his hips, pushing deeper still, and she gasped. "Oh, God, I'm so close."

"Come for me, Dana."

His eyes, now filled with heated need, reminded her of what they'd shared before. Of what she wanted to have with him always.

An explosion of pleasure burst through her and she flew straight to heaven.

Mason held her close to him, catching his breath. Fuck, that had been sexy as hell.

But now he had to get a grip on himself. He needed to keep tight control on his feelings and treat Dana like a sub.

Distance and control. That was the key.

Finally, she drew back. She gripped his shoulders and locked gazes with him, his cock still cradled in the warmth of her body.

"How did I do?"

The joyful light in her eyes made him realize he had to ramp things up. She still saw this as a fun and sexy adventure.

"Very well, but you seem to have forgotten how to properly address me."

She smiled. "How did I do, sir?"

"That's better. It's been a long day and we're both tired, so I won't punish you this time. But starting tomorrow morning, if you break a rule, I will discipline you."

She stroked his cheek with her soft hand. "Yes, sir."

He captured it and drew it away. "Stand up and gather your clothes. I'll show you where you'll be sleeping."

When she drew away, his cock slipped from her body. Instantly, he missed her warmth. He watched her lovely, naked form as she picked up her clothing. He grabbed her suitcase and she followed him down the hallway to the last door on the right. He opened it and turned on the light. She frowned as she peered inside.

"I won't be sleeping in your room?" she asked.

"No." He led her inside and placed her suitcase on the bench at the end of the bed. "You will cook breakfast for me in the morning. Have it ready by seven thirty."

He walked to the dresser and picked up the black box he'd arranged to have delivered. He opened it and took out a black leather collar.

"Lift your hair," he instructed.

She did so and he wrapped the collar around her neck and fastened it snugly. When she released her hair, he glided his hand over the silky mass, smoothing it. The sight of the collar around her neck—his collar—touched him in a way he never thought possible. He simply stared for a moment until he reclaimed his bearings.

"Once breakfast is done, go to my bedroom and wait for me outside the door." He hooked his finger through the shiny D-ring. "Naked except for this collar. And on your knees."

Her eyes widened.

"Is there a problem?" he asked.

"No, sir."

"Good." Then he walked across the room and left without looking back.

Dana walked her fingers over the thick leather of the collar as she stared after Mason. She hadn't expected to be banned to a separate room when they got here. She'd wanted to sleep in is arms, cuddled close to his solid body. To wake up with him. To make love in the morning in the sunlight.

But he called the shots and she'd agreed to that.

She glanced around the room. It wasn't a big suite like in the mansion, but it was large.

She walked into the en suite bathroom to take a shower, but stopped as she saw her reflection in the mirror. Totally naked with a black collar around her neck.

She ran her fingers over the collar again. She still remembered the feel of his fingers brushing against her skin as he'd put it on. The feel of him fastening it around her neck, then the intense look in his eyes as he'd gazed at it.

As soon as he'd put it on her, she'd felt totally possessed by him.

She turned on the water in the shower, reluctantly

took off the collar, and placed it on the vanity counter, then stepped under the stream of water.

When she finally climbed into the strange bed, she set an alarm, and pulled the covers up around her neck. She closed her eyes, wishing Mason were next to her, but quickly dropped off to sleep.

It seemed only moments later when the alarm jarred her awake. Six o'clock.

She got up and grabbed a robe from her suitcase, then went into the bathroom to get ready. Not that there was much to do since she would be greeting Mason naked. Her stomach tensed at the thought. It all seemed so strange.

How had things turned around so drastically? She had always fantasized about being with Mason, but never like this. Wearing a collar around her neck and him commanding her and . . . punishing her. She never would have dreamed it would be this way between them.

His stern manner had thrown her off-balance, and the whole situation left her uncertain.

But at the same time, it filled her with a wild sense of excitement.

Fifteen minutes later, she had bacon cooking in a pan and was mixing the dough for biscuits. When they were in the oven, she cut up some fresh fruit and made a nice fruit salad. By seven o'clock, she was washing up the dishes she'd used for preparation, then she set the table. Finally, she put the coffee on.

She glanced at the clock as she washed her hands,

then hurried to her bedroom. She fastened the collar around her neck and shed the robe. Seconds later she approached Mason's bedroom door, her stomach fluttering. She glanced around, feeling odd walking around his penthouse naked. Completely vulnerable and exposed.

She knelt down on the carpeted floor and waited.

And waited.

If felt like forever, but it was probably only five minutes, before she heard the doorknob turn. She dropped her gaze to the floor as the door opened.

Mason glanced at Dana, kneeling by his door, her gaze cast downward, and his breath caught.

Naked. Beautiful. And submissive.

His hard cock ached, as it had all night long, and excitement curled through him at the thought of dominating her. She would do anything he told her to do.

He pulled the leash from his pocket and attached it to the collar.

"Stand up." As soon as she stood up, he tugged on the leash, guiding her to the kitchen. "Breakfast is ready?"

"Yes, sir."

When they got to the kitchen, she started to walk to the oven, but he tugged her back, then marched her to the table and pushed aside the dishes and cutlery. He pressed her against the table, flattened his hand between her shoulder blades, and leaned her forward until she was bent over it. She murmured a slight protest, probably at the cold, hard tabletop against her sensitive nipples.

"Open your legs."

She widened her stance, opening her thighs.

The sight of her intimate flesh exposed to him sent his heart thumping wildly. All night, he'd longed for morning to arrive so he could find her naked and kneeling by his door. Then when he'd stepped out of his room and seen her there, just as he'd anticipated, his cock had grown hard as steel.

He had to have her.

He ran his finger over her slit. Fuck, she was already wet.

He pressed his cockhead to her folds and slid it up and down over her slickness. Then he pressed forward into her yielding flesh. He almost gasped as her warmth surrounded him.

"I'm going to fuck you now. Hard and fast. And you are not to come. Do you understand?"

"I . . . uh . . ."

He drew back a little, stroking her canal.

"Do you understand?" he snapped.

"Yes, sir."

But he was sure she didn't really. The idea of holding off her own orgasm probably confused her.

He drew back, then thrust deep into her, her hot, wet flesh surrounding him.

"Does that feel good?"

"Yes, sir."

The need in her voice heated his blood. He drew back and thrust deep again. She moaned.

He coiled his hand in her hair and pulled her head back, then thrust deep again. His fingers wrapped lightly around her neck. Then he thrust again, pleasure dancing through him.

He continued filling her with long, deep strokes. He could hear her breathing quicken, just as his did, and he could feel her pulse beating frantically against his fingertips.

"Do you like me fucking you on the table?"

"Yes, sir."

He chuckled, a release of the agitated energy that had been building in him.

He was so fucking close. Of course he was, after lusting for her all night long. He drove into her faster, like a piston, stroking her insides with long, deep strokes.

Her breathing became erratic and he could tell she was getting close.

He tugged on her hair, making her gasp.

"Do . . . not . . . come," he said sternly, as he pumped into her faster.

Then he felt it. The heat gathering in his groin, coiling tight, then . . .

Oh, God. He groaned, loud and long, as he erupted inside her sweet body.

And she moaned her release right along with him.

As soon as he finished, he pulled out, then smacked her bottom so hard it left a red mark. She gasped. Then he smacked again.

He pulled her to a standing position and marched her from the kitchen to the room at the end of the hall, her hair still wound around his hand. The Dark Room, as he called it. Because it served the needs of the darker side of his passion.

He pushed open the door and walked her across the large space to the punishment bench. He guided her to kneel on the padded ledge, then bend over. He extended her arms and cuffed her to the other end of the bench, which was sloped downward so that her ass was pushed up in the air.

Then he stood behind her and slapped her bare ass.

"Oh!" She glanced over her shoulder at him as he raised his hand. "Why are you"—she gasped as his hand slapped her ass again—"doing this?"

"I told you I would punish you if you disobeyed."

"But I didn't, I—"

He slapped again. Her ass reddened under the blows.

"I told you not to come."

"But I can't control that."

He slapped again.

"You can and you will." He slapped one final time, then stared at her bright-red ass.

Had he punished her too much, slapping her perfect round ass until it glowed?

But this was nothing compared to what Sylvie would want. Or Jenna. Or Louisa.

He unfastened the cuffs and drew her to her feet, then

guided her across the room. But the sight of her blinking back a tear tore at his heart.

He stopped and grasped her chin, then raised it. "Is this too much for you, Dana?"

It wasn't meant as a challenge, but as a genuine question.

She shook her head.

"We can stop this right now."

"No," she blurted out. "You aren't going to send me away so soon. I can do this."

"I didn't mean to—"

"I made a mistake, sir." Fire blazed in her eyes, but she dropped her gaze to the floor. "I'll do better."

He nodded. "I know you will."

He had thought he'd chain her to the wall for a while, to extend the punishment, but now he led her back to the kitchen. She served him breakfast and he had her kneel on the floor beside him as he ate. When he was finished, he ordered her to throw out the rest of the food and clean up the dishes, then join him in the living room.

He didn't know if she'd eat some of the food or just blindly follow his command and throw it all away, but she needed to find her balance in all of this.

He read his newspaper while she was busy in the kitchen, and continued reading when she entered the room. She seemed uncertain what to do. When he didn't acknowledge her presence, she finally walked to the chair he sat in and knelt down beside him, just as he'd had her do while he ate breakfast. Without lifting his gaze from the paper, he stroked her hair, like he would a favorite pet.

As time went by, she shifted from her knees and curled her legs by her side, her body resting against his leg. He kept reading the paper, but at no time did he stop being aware of her beside him.

Unable to stop himself, his hand drifted to her shoulder, then downward. He cupped her breast and stroked. Her nipple hardened to a tight bead and he squeezed it between his fingertips. She rested her head on his knee, sighing. She started to run her hand up his thigh, approaching his swollen cock, but he grabbed her wrist and drew it away.

"Do you want to be punished again?" he asked.

"No, sir." She lowered her hand.

But it was too late. The feel of her soft hand gliding along his thigh had left his cock aching with need.

He wrapped his hand around her arm and turned her toward him until she was kneeling in front of him. He unzipped his pants and pulled out his cock. Her gaze fell to his stiff flesh and she licked her lips.

"Suck it. Make me come."

"Yes, sir." She reached for him and he suppressed a groan as her delicate fingers wrapped around him. She stroked him a couple of times, then leaned forward.

At the first contact of her lips against him, he sucked in a breath. Then she swallowed his cockhead and he was immersed in her warmth. Impatient, he wrapped his hand around her head and drew her forward, filling her with his long, hard cock until she gagged. He released her, letting her draw back, but then she took him deep again.

She glided forward and back on him, watching him as she did it. Her delicate fingers cupped his tight balls and she stroked them, driving him wild. It didn't take long before he was straining to hold himself back, wanting to drive his cock deep into her throat.

She tightened her lips around his cockhead and sucked him. He groaned at the exquisite sensation.

"Fuck, make me come."

She glided down his shaft, her lips squeezing him as she went. Then she bobbed up and down in earnest, filling her mouth with him. He pivoted his hips, now fucking her mouth. Heat built inside him and he moaned, then electric sensations quivered through him and . . .

"Fuck, now. I'm going to come, baby."

He stroked her hair from her face and watched her as the heat blasted through him and he erupted into her warm mouth. He shuddered at the sweet release.

She drew back, then glided off his spent cock, still cradling it in her hand. She stroked him, her eyes turning longingly to his.

"Mason, please. I want you to make love to me."

At his hard gaze, she added, "sir."

"There are two problems with that. One, after coming twice this morning, I'm not really in any shape to do that. Two, I'm the one who calls the shots."

He stood up and pulled her to her feet, then guided her back to the Dark Room.

"You're punishing me for making a request?" she asked.

He led her to the large bureau against the side wall. "It's not a punishment really." He opened one of the small, upper drawers and pulled out a pair of jeweled nipple clamps. "Think of it more as a reminder to keep you in your place."

He drew the ring down the slender metal neck, loosening the clamp, then he placed it on her nipple. She watched, wide-eyed, as he slid the ring toward the nipple, closing the arms and pressing the rubber tips tighter around her nub.

"Ow."

"Does it hurt or are you just complaining?"

At his half-smile, she pursed her lips, hiding her own smile. "Okay, it doesn't really hurt, but it is uncomfortable."

"You'll get used to it."

She frowned, clearly having expected him to loosen it. But it was barely pressing on her, and it took time to get used to wearing clamps.

He pressed the second clamp to her other nipple and tightened it the same amount. A chain draped from one clamp to the other and he tugged on it a little.

"Ow."

"As I said, it will help you remember your place."

He tugged again, and this time she stifled her whimper.

"Now it's time for a swim."

"A swim? Where?"

He had to stop himself from laughing. At the look on her face, she must be worried he'd drag her from the apartment totally naked.

"Not too far." He led her from the Dark Room through the penthouse. Then he opened the door to his large, private terrace with a glassed-in pool.

He stripped off his clothes and dove into the water. When he surfaced, he saw her sitting at the edge of the pool.

"Should I take these off?" she asked, gesturing to the nipple rings and the leather collar around her neck.

He pursed his lips. "No, I think you should sit there, just like that."

Dana watched Mason treading water in the pool and longed to slip into the water with him, hoping he would push her against the side and take her, driving her to dizzying heights of pleasure.

This morning had been confusing and frustrating. And surprisingly exciting. Having Mason control her like this . . . denying her what she wanted while taking from her what he wanted . . . was oddly stimulating.

The collar around her neck made her feel safe and loved. She didn't know why. The nipple clamps, on the other hand, were uncomfortable. At least, they were at first. Now she was used to them. But they were unfamiliar and she wanted to take them off.

Mason swam toward her and stood in the pool waist deep. He ran his hands over her calves, which were dangling in the water. Then he glided up her thigh. He pressed her legs apart and stared at her intimate folds.

She could feel heat wash through her at his scrutiny. He pressed her feet flat against the wall of the pool and dragged her closer to the edge, until she was practically hanging over it, her legs wide open to him. He leaned forward and licked her.

"Oh." Intense pleasure swamped her senses.

But his mouth moved away from her. He smiled, then swam away. She started to slide her ass back.

"No, stay exactly where you are."

She stopped and sat in this awkward position, her feet under the water flat on the concrete wall of the pool, steadying her.

A moment later, he swam toward her again, then she felt his mouth on her. This time he glided his tongue the length of her slit, pummeling her with pleasure.

"Oh, Mason, I . . ." But she caught herself before she made the same mistake.

His mouth moved away and his gaze locked on hers.

"I mean, thank you, sir."

He laughed, then pressed his face to her folds again and covered her flesh with his hot mouth. His tongue worked at her, sending a heated frenzy through her. He teased her clit and she moaned, feeling the pleasure cascade through her. His fingers glided inside her and he stroked her passage. The heat built within her and she could feel an orgasm building.

She arched against him and he drove his fingers deep, while he tongued her clit.

Oh, she could feel it approaching, that delicious promise of release.

She arched again but as the sweetness of the pleasure cocooned her, he grabbed her waist and pulled her into the water. Her feet hit the bottom and she stood waist deep, the cool water surrounding her heated, intimate flesh.

He shoved her against the side of the pool and his big cock drove into her, pinning her to the concrete.

His arms tightened around her, pulling her close to his hard, wet body, but only from the waist down, careful not to crush her clamped nipples against him.

He pulled back and plunged his cock deep into her again. After his intimate attention, her body was eager and ready. He thrust a few more times, then pressed his lips to her ear.

"Are you close?"

She nodded enthusiastically. "Oh, yes, sir."

"Good. Now show me how willing and able you are to do what I tell you. I'm going to keep fucking you, but you are not to come."

She couldn't help groaning.

He thrust into her again, his big, hard cock stretching her. He picked up speed, hammering into her, his cock sending wild, tingling sensations through her with each stroke. It was pure torture feeling the pleasure build in her and fighting it back. But she was determined to survive this. To hold off the orgasm she so desperately wanted. Because she wanted Mason more. And to have him, she had to prove that she could meet his needs. That she could follow whatever command he gave her.

He pounded into her and she whimpered at the joyful sensations building in her. He tugged on the chain dangling from her breasts, and she yipped at the pinch of the clamps.

Then he thrust forward, grinding his pelvis against hers.

At the flood of heat inside her, she had to fight back the rising orgasm with every cell of her being. Just barely stopping short before flying over the edge.

He groaned and she held her breath, squeezing him between her legs, desperately fighting the onslaught of pleasure.

Finally, he drew back and his cock slipped from between her legs. She moaned in disappointment.

He tipped up her chin and smiled at her.

"Good girl." Then he kissed her, his lips moving gently on hers in a sweet, loving kiss.

Then it was over.

"Now go make me some lunch."

After lunch, Mason went to his exercise room to work out, then returned, showered and smelling wonderful. For the rest of the afternoon, he read, with her on the leather couch beside him, his hands casually stroking her. Sometimes just a glide over her hip, or arm. Sometimes, slipping between her legs and teasing her to distraction. He spent hours doing that and by the time evening rolled around, she was desperate to be fucked.

"Sir, may I ask you a question?"

He glanced up from his book. "All right."

"When are you going to fuck me?"

He smiled. "Not today."

"Oh." Disappointment lurched through her.

He laughed then slipped down to his knees. He released one of the nipple clamps and she tensed at the sharp sensation that burst through her tender nub, but he immediately covered it with his mouth. The intensity of the pleasure as he suckled caused her to gasp. He licked and sucked until she was filled with an agony of pleasure.

Then he kissed down her belly to her mound. When his tongue found her clit and he teased it, she leaned back on the couch, ready for the release she had been yearning for.

But after a few sweeps of his tongue, he leaned back and replaced the clamp on her nipple, then stood up.

"Let's go get some dinner."

She frowned. "Mason, wait."

He arched an eyebrow. "Are you refusing me?"

"No, sir. I just . . . want to understand."

He sat down on the chair facing her and leaned forward. "That's fair."

"Why are you doing this? Tormenting me like this? I

mean, I knew you were going to order me to do things, and I will gladly do them. But I thought we'd be together . . . have sex. That I'd please you and . . . you know . . . that . . . well, that we'd find pleasure together."

"You want me to fuck you, but this is about you learning discipline and following orders."

"And being punished?"

"Yes, and we've hardly done any of that."

She frowned and pointed at a nipple clamp. "What about these?"

His eyebrow arched again. "Really? You think that's a punishment?"

Ever since they'd started talking about her submitting to him, Mason had grown increasingly distant. But she'd thought they had started closing that distance just a little. Yet now the gap between them seemed to grow to a deep chasm.

"If you think that's a punishment, you really understand nothing. I want you to get a true idea of what I need, yet what I've shown you today barely scratches the surface. These . . ." He tugged on the chain attached to her nipple clamps, making her gasp. "These are for pleasure."

"But they hurt," she protested.

"Do they really?" He grasped one clamp and adjusted the tiny ring.

She sucked in a breath at the increased pressure.

"Maybe that hurts." He squeezed it tighter still, making her eyes water at the painful sensation. "Does it?"

She nodded.

His lips compressed. "Do you want me to loosen it?"

She sucked in a breath, but shook her head. She would show him. A little pain wouldn't scare her away. If he was trying to drive her away before the end of the trial period, he'd have to do better than this.

Then she felt the other nipple clamp tightened and she fought back the tears welling in her eyes.

"You wouldn't want them unbalanced, would you?"

"No, sir."

He leaned back in the chair. "Look, Dana, I'm just showing you what it would be like. I'm used to women who like this kind of thing. I meant it when I said this would be nothing to my current subs. Fuck, you wouldn't believe what some of them want."

"Like what?"

"You really want to know?"

When she nodded, he grabbed her hand, led her across the living room to his den, and sat her down in front of his computer. He rolled up another chair and opened his browser. He pulled up an image of a woman's backside with dark red welts across it.

"I have one sub who wants me to hit her so hard that it will scar."

Dana stared at the picture in disbelief. How could anyone actually want that?

Then he brought up another picture, of a woman with a rope coiled intricately around her body, holding her tightly bound. But what drew Dana's attention . . .

what she couldn't drag her gaze away from . . . were her breasts.

"One sub wanted to be bound so tight . . . Well, you can see."

The rope was wound so tightly around her breasts that they were deep purple.

"She really wanted that?"

He shrugged. "Everyone has their own needs." He shook his head. "I didn't have a taste for it, though, so I ended it with her."

She was relieved to know that Mason didn't want to take part in something so extreme.

"Was there anything else you refused a sub for?"

He narrowed his eyes as he thought about it. "There was one sub who wanted to take on four men at once."

"What do you mean, 'take on'?"

"I mean she wanted all of them inside her at once."

"But . . . how . . . ?"

"Well, her mouth, of course. And have you heard of double penetration?"

She shook her head.

"You can probably figure out what it means, right?"

"One man in . . . uh . . . front, and the other behind her?" The thought was unsettling.

"That's right. But with four men . . . well, with some careful positioning, and a little patience, a woman can actually take two cocks inside her vagina at the same time."

Suddenly, an image formed in her mind. A woman

sitting on a man's lap, his cock inside her ass, then two men kneeling in front of her, somehow pushing both their cocks into her vagina. At the same time, another man standing beside her, pressing his cock into her mouth.

"Did you do that?"

He nodded. "I had to try it. But I prefer just two men with a woman. Simple and yet still intensely erotic."

"Does that mean you want me to be with another man?" she asked, uncertainty gripping her. Was that something she'd be willing to do?

"Dana, you don't have to do any of this. I told you, I don't think this is for you. Any of it."

"I just . . . I'm not sure about any of this, but I'm willing to try." She bit her lip. "Please just be patient with me."

Mason sighed deeply and stood up. "I think it's time you go to bed."

"But it's only eight o'clock."

"You can read. Now go."

She stood up. "Yes, sir."

She scooted off to her room and closed the door behind her. Then she leaned against it, uncertain. Wishing she hadn't displeased him.

Mason watched her go, his stomach in knots. He hated this. She was trying so hard. Damn it, why didn't she just give up so they could be done with this?

But he hadn't really pushed her hard enough to make her give up. A little deprivation wouldn't be daunting enough for Dana. She was sweet, and young, and innocent. But she was also strong willed, and determined to achieve whatever she set her mind to.

And he'd given her a challenge. She was not about to give up easily.

He grabbed the decanter of scotch, poured himself a glass, and stared out at the city lights. Fuck, everything else aside, he regretted leaving her wanting tonight. He had taken his pleasure from her so many times today and he wanted so much to give her the same in return. He wanted to feel her clamping around him as she shuddered in orgasm.

He longed to have her here in his arms. To drive himself deep into her body.

To hear her scream his name as she came.

He sucked back the liquor and turned on a movie. But even though it was an action suspense, it couldn't keep his attention. He paced the room, then settled down and poured another drink.

When the movie ended, he turned on another. His thoughts swirled around and around. How had he found himself in this crazy position? Trying to drive Dana away, when all he wanted was to fuck her again and again. Hell, how could he have allowed himself to wind up fucking her in the first place?

When the second movie ended, he stood up and headed to his bedroom. At least, that had been his intent, but he found himself at Dana's door.

He turned the knob and pushed the door open. The room was dark.

He stepped inside and closed the door behind him.

"Is that you, Mason?" Dana's voice was small and hoarse in the darkness. As his eyes adjusted to the soft moonlight streaming in the window, he could make out her form on the bed.

"You mean 'sir.' "

"Yes, I'm sorry. Is that you, sir?"

"Fuck, of course it is."

He walked toward the bed, then pulled the covers back, exposing her naked body. His cock jolted to attention.

"You are so fucking hot."

She gazed up at him with wide eyes. "Thank you, sir."

He stripped off his clothes, dropping them to the floor piece by piece. Then he knelt on the bed and prowled over her. He lowered his body onto her, the feel of her warm, silky skin beneath him lighting a fire within.

His mouth found hers and his tongue slid inside. Her tongue tangled with his. His hand found her breast and she whimpered softly.

"Fuck, I need you, baby."

He found her throat and kissed it, loving her murmurs of approval.

Her hand wrapped around his cock and her touch set his desire ablaze.

"Please, sir, I need you inside me."

She squeezed and dragged his cockhead over her moist, intimate flesh, then centered him on her opening.

She nuzzled his neck. "Please."

"Aw, fuck." He drove forward, impaling her in one stroke.

She gasped, then wrapped her legs around him, opening to him.

He drew back and thrust even deeper this time.

She gasped again, clinging to his shoulders.

"Oh, yes."

He began to thrust with a steady rhythm. Deep into her body. Loving her moans of pleasure.

"Do you like this, Dana?"

"Yes, sir. Yes. Please fuck me."

"Oh, God damn."

He rode her faster, ramming his cock into her hard.

She arched against him, encouraging.

"Oh, please," she whimpered. "I'm so close."

"Me, too, baby. But I won't come until you do."

He drove into her like a jackhammer, determined to drive her to a mind-shattering orgasm.

"Oh, yes, oh, yes . . . oh, God." Her voice grew higher and higher with each word.

He felt her tighten around him and she arched upward.

"Yes, sir. I'm . . . "

She moaned. "Oh, Mason . . ." She moaned against his ear, setting his blood boiling.

She trembled in his arms, then shuddered her release.

He drove deep, then let go of his control and kept driving into her until he felt the burn in his groin. Then the explosion of heat and . . .

He jerked against her, erupting inside her soft, accepting body.

Her waning orgasm seemed to burst back to life and he kept on pumping as she moaned with another orgasm.

Finally, she collapsed on the bed, clinging to him. He was worried about his weight on her, but when he tried to shift up to his elbows, she clung tightly to him.

He couldn't help it. He laughed in sheer joy. Then he swept her into his arms, carried her to his bedroom, and pulled her into his bed. He held her tightly to him, his arms possessively around her. Then he fell asleep.

Mason woke up to the feel of Dana's soft body pressed close to him. His arms were around her and her soft breast was cupped in his hand.

Damn, she was never supposed to be in his bed. But, fuck, he'd had a few drinks last night, struggling with what he had to do to prove to her she didn't want this lifestyle, and he'd lost his focus. He'd given her exactly what she wanted, and shown that no matter how hard he was on her, she'd have the sweet prize at the end of the day. That didn't help his case.

The soft vibration of his phone on the bedside table drew his attention. Carefully, he shifted away from Dana, trying not to wake her, and picked it up.

"Mason here," he said quietly.

"What the fuck, man! You're screwing your sister?" Guy said.

"What are you talking about?" Mason sat on the side of the bed and rubbed his face, then glanced back at Dana as he stood up. She continued sleeping peacefully.

He walked across the room as his friend continued talking, then slipped out the door.

"Hey, man, I'm not one to judge, but if you're going to do it, at least don't get it splattered across the media."

Mason closed the door behind him.

"Send me the links," he said. "And she's not my sister, she's my stepsister."

"Yeah, that is so much better," Guy said with sarcasm.

"I thought you said you weren't judging."

Guy chuckled. "Hey, I gotta yank your chain every now and again. But seriously, man, this is not good for your business. And what's your father going to say?"

"It's my father who leaked it. He's trying to punish me."

"Ha ha. Just like you're punishing your little sister, right? I bet you're yanking *her* chains."

"Okay, drop it, Guy. I have enough trouble right now. I don't need crap from you."

"All right. Look, though, if there's anything I can do to help . . ."

"Yeah, thanks. I might take you up on that. But right now, I just want those links."

"I sent a few, but it's all over the papers and the Internet. Not exactly hard to find."

"I'll check it out. Thanks."

Mason flicked off his phone and headed for the den. He opened his e-mail and clicked on the first link Guy had sent him, then the next. His stomach clenched. His father had really gone all out, making it look like Dana was actually his sister. Some papers had checked their facts and reported her as his stepsister, but it still looked bad. Mason's main business interests were privately owned, so he wouldn't be affected by dropping stock prices, but there would be companies who would refuse to do business with him because of this. Especially with how sleazy the articles made it sound. He knew he could weather it, though.

He wasn't so sure about Dana.

"Mason?"

His head jerked up and he saw Dana standing in the doorway of his den. She was naked, with her collar around her neck. The sight of her made his cock swell.

"Dana, go kneel by my door and wait like you're supposed to."

"I'm sorry, sir, but I woke up and you were gone. I wasn't sure—"

"I said go," he said sternly. "And put on the nipple clamps."

She pouted, but nodded and turned. The sight of her delightfully round, naked ass sent his cock twitching.

He needed to pay attention to this scandal. To read

the articles, and check his inbox for the e-mails that were bound to flood in. But he had to keep pushing Dana, too.

He closed his browser and walked out the door. The sight of her kneeling by his door filled him with need.

"You were in my bed this morning."

"Yes, sir."

"But that's against the rules."

She lifted her head, gazing at him in disbelief. "But you brought me there last night."

"Are you saying I'm to blame?"

Confusion filled her eyes. "Not to blame, no, but I didn't think I did anything wrong."

"You broke the rules. It doesn't matter why."

"But . . . I'm not supposed to say no to you. You shouldn't punish me for—"

"Let's get this straight, Dana. There is no *shouldn't* where I'm concerned. I can punish you for anything I want. Anytime. I can punish you for nothing at all."

She bowed her head again. "Yes, sir."

"Follow me."

He led her to the Dark Room. Once inside, he sat her in the large, wooden restraint chair and fastened her wrists to the armrests. He wrapped the leather waist strap around her and buckled it, then attached her ankles to the rings anchored to the floor, wide apart from each other. Then he retrieved a ball gag and put it in her mouth and fastened it in place.

"I'm going to leave you like this, but I will be watching you on my monitor, through that camera there." He turned and pointed at the camera on the wall. "So you aren't alone. If you want this to stop, tap your fingers several times, then stop, then do it again. Keep repeating that and I'll come and let you loose."

She gazed at him with her big, blue eyes. He could tell she knew that if she gave that signal, she would be giving up.

"You understand?"

She nodded, then dragged her gaze from his.

He left the room, feeling guilty, but he needed to keep on top of the brewing scandal. And he needed to keep pushing her. This allowed him to do both.

He returned to his den and opened his browser again. After a sickening forty minutes of reading blogs and newspaper articles, along with nasty e-mails from so-called friends and business connections, he closed his browser. He needed to take action. He picked up the phone and called Guy.

"It's Mason," he said when Guy answered. "I have some stocks to buy."

"You're going after your father's company."

"You bet. And I could use your help."

Dana sat in the hard chair, her mouth stretched around the rubber ball—and tried to stay calm. She glanced at the camera Mason had pointed to, reminding herself she was not alone, that he was watching her. That he was there if she needed him.

But she felt so alone. And a little frightened at being bound like this. Her stomach had clenched as soon as Mason had left the room and it was still tight as a drum. And it ached.

She blinked, staring at the camera and trying to picture Mason watching her from his den. Thinking that he cared about her and was only trying to make her understand.

But she didn't understand. Why did he like this kind of thing?

Much of what he'd done with her yesterday she'd actually found exhilarating, and highly erotic. But the punishment? She wasn't sure about that.

And this . . . she knew she didn't like this. Bound and left alone in a room. Feeling totally helpless. If Mason had been here in the same room with her, she would have felt safe, but . . .

Panic welled up inside her. What if something had happened to Mason? What if he'd forgotten about her? If he'd gone out somewhere?

No, he wouldn't do that.

But she didn't know for sure. She was here alone. All alone!

Tears welled in her eyes, but she blinked them back. She couldn't give up. She felt her fingers growing tense. She had to stop them from tapping.

She wanted this to stop. She wanted him to come back.

All she had to do was tap her fingers.

But that would be admitting defeat. That would mean she would lose Mason forever.

Oh, God, how long could she hold out?

Mason hung up the phone, having set the ball in motion.

He glanced at Dana on the monitor. Concern washed through him as he saw her tense expression.

He checked the clock and realized . . . fuck, he'd left her alone for almost two hours.

He shot to his feet and marched to the Dark Room, then opened the door. The feeling of her tension . . . and fear . . . filled the room. He strode to the chair and released her wrists, then unfastened the ball gag. She didn't look at him. He unfastened the other restraints then took her hand and helped her to her feet.

Then he saw it. The tears welling in her eyes.

"Dana, I—"

A whimper escaped her throat, stopping his words. Then the tears began to flow freely.

"I was frightened," she murmured. Still she wouldn't look at him.

"You left me here alone and I was . . ." Her words ended in a sob.

"Dana, I'm so sorry."

He pulled her into his arms and she rested against him, but she did not wrap her arms around him like she usually did. In a strange way, that made him feel rejected.

Just as she must have felt being locked away in here.

He stroked her hair, feeling the tears spill onto his shirt.

He scooped her up and carried her from the room. He wanted to hold her close. To tell her how much he loved her. To reassure her and tell her everything would be all right.

But it wouldn't. And he had to be strong.

He had to drive her away from him.

With this scandal, she would be better off in Paris.

If she was this affected by being bound in the chair, but still hadn't chosen to end it, he knew he had to do something drastic to finally convince her that she couldn't accept being his sub. Something extreme that would push her past her limit.

An idea came to mind and he almost rejected it immediately, because he found it repugnant. But aside from beating her to her limit, which he would not do, it was the only arrow left in his quiver.

Mason gazed at Dana, who now rested quietly on the couch in his den, her breathing deep and even. He'd settled her down there, reassuring her he wouldn't leave her again, and covered her with the soft, cashmere throw. Finally, she'd fallen asleep.

He picked up his phone and tapped in a text to one of his subs, making arrangements for this evening.

When Dana awoke an hour later, Mason walked to the couch and sat beside her.

"Feel better now?"

She nodded.

He tipped up her chin. "You could have given the signal."

"I know."

"Why didn't you?"

"Maybe I was a little afraid that I would give it and you wouldn't come."

"Of course I would have come."

She nodded. "But more . . ." She locked gazes with him. "I won't give up on you. I know we can make this work. I just have to prove it to you."

"And I don't agree. But you know that." He sighed. "Okay, so I'm going to have to up the ante. I am going to give you a challenge, and you need to decide if you want to go ahead with it or just end this now."

"What is it?"

Mason's steel-blue gaze bored into her, assessing. A shiver raced down her spine.

"I want to watch you with another man."

His words caught her totally off guard.

"What?" she blurted out in disbelief.

"I am going to order you to be with another man and I'm going to watch."

"I don't believe you."

He raised an eyebrow. "Really? And why is that?"

"You've protected me. You didn't want to take my virginity. I can't believe you'd allow another man to touch me."

She thought she saw a flicker of uncertainty in his gaze, but it could have just been because that's what she wanted to see.

"Don't get me wrong, Dana. I will still protect you. Always. But you are no longer a virgin, and once we're done, you will have other men in your life."

She hated that he still insisted this would end.

"But those would be men I choose. Not one that I have no say in choosing."

"But remember, you were willing to sell your virginity to someone you didn't know. So clearly, this isn't outside your comfort zone."

Was he kidding? Of course it was outside her comfort zone. But it was true she'd been willing to have sex with a stranger, so he could reasonably ask her—command her—to do so for him.

But her stomach knotted at the thought.

Maybe Mason was bluffing.

"Is this enough to make you finally give in? Or do we proceed?"

She lowered her gaze. "I will do what you ask, sir."

"Really?" He sighed and stood up. "All right. Arrangements have already been made. Meet me in the Dark Room at seven p.m. Right now I suggest you get some food to keep up your strength, then go to your room and put on the outfit I will lay out for you."

"Yes, sir."

Mason stood up and left the office. She checked the clock and realized she had an hour and a half. She stood up, clinging to the throw, and went to her room to find a robe. Then she went to the kitchen to find something to eat.

Dana walked toward the Dark Room wearing her collar and a harness of leather straps that crisscrossed her body, but covered nothing. Around her wrists and ankles she wore leather cuffs with silver rings attached, and she had on glossy, black patent stiletto pumps.

She opened the door and peered inside. Mason wasn't here yet.

Nor was anyone else.

Her stomach quaked at the thought. Surely Mason didn't really intend to bring another man here.

She walked into the room, a little uncertain as to what to do, so she knelt on the floor to wait.

Moments later, the door opened. Mason smiled at her approvingly as he stepped inside.

"Very good." He walked across the room to a padded bench. "Now come over here."

She stood up, being careful on the high, narrow heels. She wasn't used to heels this high, or this narrow, so she walked toward him with as much grace as she could manage.

The bench, which was about eighteen inches wide, was upholstered with burgundy leather.

"Sit in the middle of the bench," he instructed.

She sat down.

"No, I mean straddle it."

"Oh." She lifted her leg over it and sat with the bench between her legs, the leather smooth and cool against her intimate flesh. He lowered two thick chains from the ceiling until they dangled in front of her. On the ends were black handles, like on a bicycle handlebar.

"Grab the grips," he said.

She wrapped her hands around them. They had some give and were comfortable to hold. Mason flicked a clip through the ring on one of her wrists and attached it to the chain, then did the same with the other wrist. He walked behind her and she felt the chains pulling upward, drawing her hands above her head. They stopped before her arms were pulled totally straight.

"Now I'm going to blindfold you."

A black cloth glided across her face and Mason tied it behind her head, leaving her in darkness.

"Is that comfortable?" he asked.

"Yes, sir."

"Good. Now I'll bring in James."

"Mason, I—" The words had just tumbled from her mouth before she could stop them. She bit her lip.

"Yes, Dana?" His voice came from a couple of yards away. "Do you want to stop this?"

And admit defeat. He didn't say it, but it's what he meant.

"I . . . No, I'm just . . . a little nervous."

"That's not surprising, but I'm glad you don't want to stop. I wanted you to at first, but the more I've thought about it, the more I realized I was looking forward to it."

Confusion raced through her. But this must mean . . . He was going to pretend. The blindfold. His excitement. It had to be that he was going to pretend.

"Ready?" he asked.

"I . . . guess so."

She heard the door open. She couldn't hear footsteps on the carpeted floor, but she sensed him walking closer. Nervousness fluttered through her.

She felt him sit down on the upholstered bench in front of her. She could feel his gaze on her, heating her skin. Her nipples puckered as goose bumps danced across her flesh.

At the light brush of fingertips across her knee, she sucked in a breath.

The width of the bench between her legs kept her thighs open so her intimate flesh was exposed to him. His fingers moved slowly up her thigh, gliding over her sensitive flesh.

Her stomach tightened and she became intensely aware of the thumping of her heart. The coarseness of her breathing. And when his fingers approached her intimate folds, the small, strangled murmur that escaped her lips.

Then his fingers brushed over her there and . . . Oh, God, she trembled at his touch. As his fingers stroked lightly over her folds, his touch seemed different.

But of course he wanted to make this seem real.

She was drenched with wanting him, and he could feel it. If this had truly been a stranger, she would have been embarrassed by how quickly she was turned on.

He stroked over her slick flesh and she murmured softly, opening her legs a little more.

"Do you like that, Dana?"

She gasped at the sound of Mason's voice from across the room, and clamped her legs tightly against the bench.

"Mason?"

He chuckled. "You thought it was really me touching you?"

"Yes, I—" She sucked in air as the strange fingers stroked over her again. "Who is—?"

"I told you. His name is James. He's one of my subs."

"Your subs? But . . ." She shook her head in confusion. "You like men?"

He laughed. "No, that's not my taste. But watching James touching one of my female subs . . . under my control, of course . . . Watching him fuck her . . . I find that exciting."

James' fingers moved over her again. His touch was so foreign yet . . . felt so good.

Then his fingers slid away. She held her breath, waiting for what would happen next. Then the brush of raspy skin on her inner thigh startled her and she gasped.

"It's all right, Dana. James is going to touch you with his mouth now."

She felt goose bumps spread across her skin. The thought of a strange man . . . his mouth touching her there.

His warm tongue brushed across her folds and she jerked back in the little space she had.

"Mason, I . . ." Her voice quivered. "I don't know if I can . . ."

She could feel James' breath on her sensitive flesh, but he didn't move closer.

"Are you sure, Dana?" Mason's voice drew closer.

Then she felt him sit on the bench behind her, close to her.

"We'll stop if you want, but . . ." His hand rested on her naked shoulder and his lips brushed the back of her neck. "I think you'll enjoy it if you give it a chance."

She knew she could say no, and she should. But then she would lose her last chance to have a life with Mason.

She hesitated. Mason stroked her shoulders, his light touch sending delightful shivers through her. Then he cupped her breasts, the warmth of his big hands around her taking her breath away.

She drew in several deep breaths and thought about the other man leaning forward and licking her. Pleasuring her in such an intimate place. A place that only Mason had been until now.

The thought that it would please Mason made her want to do it.

No, it wasn't just that. *She* wanted to feel it. This stranger giving her pleasure when she couldn't even see his face. With Mason close behind her. Watching. Oh, God, it was so kinky and . . . her reaction to it so surprising.

Mason stroked her hair to one side and his lips brushed her skin again, sending the fine hairs along her neck to full attention.

"So . . . ?" he queried.

She nodded. "Yes, sir. Please, let's continue."

He chuckled, then nuzzled her neck.

She felt his head nod and then James' warm tongue brushed against her intimate flesh.

"Do you like that, Dana?" Mason murmured in her ear.

"Yes," she whimpered.

The stranger's fingers glided over her slick flesh, then two of them slid inside her. Now that she was committed, she just let the pleasure singe her. She arched against his questing mouth as he glided his tongue along her folds, and dropped her head back on Mason's shoulder.

James found her clit and shimmied his tongue over it. Pleasure wafted through her.

Mason stroked her breasts, then slid his fingertips over her nipples, lightly teasing at first. Then he pinched them, sending pleasure spiking through her.

His lips caressed her neck and James' tongue teased her sensitive bundle of nerves. His fingers moved inside her, thrusting now as his mouth drove her to higher levels of joyful sensations.

"Let it go, Dana," Mason murmured against her ear, then he squeezed her nipples again. "Come for us."

For us.

"Oh, God." She arched against James' determined mouth and he suckled as his fingers thrust inside her over and over again. Pure joy blasted through her, carrying her to the edge of forever.

Her fingers tightened around the grips as she moaned, her head pushing back against Mason as his lips brushed her cheek.

Finally, the orgasm waned and she slumped, gasping for air.

Mason kissed her cheek.

"You see. You did enjoy that."

"Yes, sir."

"Now it's your turn to thank James."

She felt hard, rigid flesh brush against her cheek.

"Open your mouth," Mason commanded softly.

She opened it and the hot, hard flesh brushed her lips then pushed inside her mouth. She closed around it. James' cock slid deeper into her. Slowly, but relentlessly, until his whole, impressive length was inside her.

Then he glided back, her lips caressing his long, thick shaft. With only the tip of him in her mouth, she swirled her tongue over him, then around the ridge of his cock-head.

"Fuck, I love watching James' big dick in your mouth." Mason's words wisped against her ear. "Suck on him, baby."

James slid forward again, but stopped partway and she began to suck.

Mason kissed her cheek. His breath brushed against her mouth and James' big cock. The thought of Mason's mouth so close to another man's erection sent wild tremors through her. God, she was getting even wetter.

She continued to suck James, her hands tightening around the grips, wishing it was James' cock being squeezed within her fingers.

She heard a groan. From James. She drove deep on his cock, then bobbed forward and back, his hard flesh gliding between her lips. She sucked him again and she could feel his body tense in front of her.

"Fuck!" It was the first time she'd heard James' voice. Deep and silky, though coarsened by his need.

Then he erupted inside her mouth.

She continued to lick his shaft and he murmured in appreciation, then he drew back, his big cock slipping from her. Mason's face was still beside hers and she leaned back against him.

"You liked that," he murmured against her ear, his breath sending tingles along her neck.

"Yes, sir," she sighed.

His hand cupped her breasts and he squeezed gently, then his fingers found her hard nipples.

Her inner passage ached with need as she arched her hips forward against nothingness. She couldn't see James but she could sense him in front of her. Looking at her naked body.

"Mason . . . sir . . . Please . . ." She arched again. "I

want to feel his big cock inside me. I want him to fuck me . . . while you watch."

Mason's hands cupped her breasts, drawing her tight to his chest. "Dana, I don't think—"

"Please!" She arched against his hands. "I *need* him inside me." The desperation in her voice surprised even her. "Please, sir. You want to watch him fuck me. And I want you to see it. I want you to see him make me come."

"Because you want him?"

She shook her head. "Because I want to please you. I want you to see him slide in and out of me. To bring me to pleasure. Knowing we're both doing it to please you."

To her surprise, Mason chuckled. Then his lips brushed against her temple. "Fuck, baby, you are good. But after your talented mouth got him off, James isn't really in any shape to fuck you."

Disappointment washed through her that Mason would not allow this. The longing to feel this other man's cock inside her body was indescribably potent.

She felt Mason's fingers trail along the side of her wrist, then the restraint loosened. He freed her other wrist, too, then wrapped his hands around hers, enveloping them. He drew them to the bench then . . .

"Oh." She felt hot flesh against her palm and Mason wrapped her fingers around it.

James' semi-erect cock.

"You'll have to help him."

Oh, God, Mason's hands were wrapped around hers

as her fingers were wrapped around James's swelling cock. Mason guided her hand up and down to stroke James. But he didn't release her. So they stroked James together. Both her and Mason squeezing James's now-pulsing erection.

"It's so big," she murmured.

"Yes, it is," Mason agreed. "And soon it's going to be inside you."

"Oh, God, yes."

"Would you like James to talk to you, Dana?"

She squeezed the big cock in her hand and realized she did.

"Yes, sir, I would."

"Go ahead, James."

"Hello, Dana."

Oh, God, hearing his voice . . . deep, silky . . . sexy— talking to her—changed everything. Suddenly, he was no longer just a presence in the room. A mouth. A pair of hands.

A cock.

"Hello, James," she said tremulously.

Mason drew her hands from James' cock and lifted them to James' chest. Her hands glided along the muscular planes of this stranger, still guided by Mason.

"I like you touching me," the seductive voice— James—said.

He was a man. Strong. Muscular. And he was going to fuck her.

Mason swirled her hands over James' chest, then down

his tight, sculpted abs. The hot, hard tip of his cock brushed against the back of her hand, then Mason pressed her hands to it again. She wrapped her fingers around the erection and Mason released her.

"It feels good with your hand around my cock, Dana."

A quiver fluttered through her.

He leaned forward and nuzzled her neck, then his hand cupped her breast.

"I can hardly wait to be inside you. To drive my hard cock into you and make you come again."

"Oh, yes," she murmured, yearning for the same thing.

James slid closer to her, then he drew her hand from his shaft and pressed the big cockhead against her slick opening.

God, she wanted this so much but . . . it felt wrong. To let James push his big cock into her. She was Mason's, and his alone. Another man shouldn't be inside her body . . .

Unless . . .

As James started to press forward, she pressed her hand to his chest. "Wait."

"What is it, Dana?" Mason asked, his body still pressed tight to her back.

"I can't just let him fuck me."

"You want to stop?" Mason asked.

She shook her head. "I . . ." She arched back against Mason, feeling his cock hard and thick against her. "I want you inside me, too."

He let out a sharp breath. "Do you know what you're asking?"

"Yes, I want you to . . . um . . . take me from behind. To take my . . . uh . . . back opening virginity."

He laughed. "Your back opening virginity?"

She giggled and nodded. "I don't know what to call it. My ass virginity? Anal virginity?"

Mason chuckled again.

"But . . . Please, Mason. I want to feel you there. To have you inside me when James fucks me."

He drew her tight and kissed her temple. "Fuck, baby, you're full of surprises."

She felt him nod and he moved away as James wrapped his hands around her shoulders and drew her toward him.

"Stand up, Dana," James instructed. "Then lean toward me. I'll keep you steady."

She stood up, the bench between her legs, and leaned toward James. He held her steady so she didn't lose her balance in the darkness of the blindfold.

She felt Mason move close behind her, then his fingers, slippery with warm gel, stroked over her ass, between her cheeks. Then he pressed against her opening. One slick finger slid into her. She rested her head on James' shoulder as Mason moved his finger inside her. Stroking her tight, virgin passage. Soon, he slid a second finger inside, stretching her.

"It'll be tight at first, but he's stretching you. Making you ready," James reassured.

When Mason's third finger slid inside, it felt uncomfortably tight, but she kept still, letting him stroke inside her.

After a few moments, his fingers left her body. She felt relieved, but still needy.

When she felt his big cockhead, as slick as his fingers had been, press between her cheeks and glide over her opening, she tensed.

"I'm going to push inside you now. Just relax."

James rubbed her shoulders, calming her a little.

Mason began to push forward. She tensed again.

"Dana, do you want me to stop?" Mason asked patiently.

"No, sir." She forced herself to relax, even as his impossibly big cockhead rested tightly against her.

He began to press forward again and she willed herself not to tense. His hot flesh stretched her, opening her up. Then he slowly pushed into her.

"Does it hurt?" Mason asked.

She nodded. "But please don't stop."

He pushed deeper, his cockhead stretching her wider. The pain increased, but she wanted this so much she didn't care.

"Oh, Mason."

He was relentless, slowly pushing his thick flesh into her. Then his big cockhead was all the way in and he stopped, giving her a rest. The pain eased and she realized it was her tension making it worse. She relaxed, leaning her head on James' shoulder, feeling his breath against her neck. A ripple of pleasure quivered through her.

She wanted Mason deeper.

"More, sir."

Mason pressed forward, sliding his thick cock deeper inside her.

"Oh, you're so big." When he slowed, she cried, "Please keep going."

The big shaft moved deeper. She couldn't believe how much she stretched around him, and now that she focused on staying relaxed . . . it felt good.

Then she felt his body tight against hers. He was all the way in.

He wrapped his hands around her waist and drew her torso up until she was standing in front of him. His arms wrapped around her and he kissed her neck, his lips playing against her skin in a light dance of passion.

"You're so beautiful . . . and I can't describe how fucking hot it is being inside your ass."

He guided her downward until he was sitting on the bench, leaning back enough so her ass perched on his groin, his cock embedded deep inside her.

She reached forward, her hands seeking James. He took her hands and guided them to his cock.

"Is this what you're looking for?" he asked as she wrapped both hands around his rock-hard member.

"Yes." God, his sexy voice sent scorching need fluttering through her.

She squeezed him, then stroked. Mason's big cock twitched inside her.

"Please, James. Fuck me now."

James moved closer, then she felt his cockhead brush against her tender, aching flesh.

"You want me inside you?"

"Yes. Oh, please, yes."

Then he drove forward, impaling her with one deep stroke.

She gasped, totally aware of the two big cocks filling her. The two hard, hot bodies sandwiching her tight between them.

"Oh, God." Tears filled her eyes. "This feels so . . . incredible."

"Fuck her, James," Mason ordered, his voice tight with need.

James obeyed his master immediately, drawing back, then thrusting deep into Dana. She gasped at the intense pleasure, James' strokes augmented by the feel of Mason deep inside her ass.

James drew back and drove deep again.

Mason cupped her breasts, caressing them as James drove into her again. And again.

She arched, causing her to shift on Mason's cock, making her gasp again.

"Fuck her hard and fast," Mason instructed, his words ragged.

James picked up speed, driving deep and hard like a jackhammer.

Every time he drove into her, she was aware of Mason's thick cock deep inside her, too. But Mason kept still while James pumped into her.

The incredible pleasure that had been slowly building blasted through her like a geyser and she moaned.

"Is he making you come, Dana?"

She nodded at Mason's words.

He gripped her chin, tipping it back until she rested on his shoulder, James' insatiable cock driving into her over and over again.

"Tell me. Use his name."

"James is making me come, he . . . Ohhh," she moaned as James thrust incredibly deep.

Her body quivered, and she felt it.

"Yes, I'm coming." She threw her head back against Mason's shoulder. "James, you're . . . ahhh . . . making me come."

Then she shattered. The orgasm claiming her with such force that she trembled against Mason's body, tears streaming from her eyes.

James groaned and his cock pulsed inside her, then she felt the heat of his semen flooding her.

She sucked in air, and her ragged breaths sounded almost like sobs.

She was crushed tight between the two men, Mason's cock still incredibly hard inside her, and James' still a presence inside her, too.

Suddenly, Mason pressed her forward, her body covering James'. James wrapped his arms around her and held her close. Mason wrapped his hands around her hips and she felt his cock stroke the length of her passage as he drew back, then he slowly pushed forward again, filling her with his marble-hard member. He drew back, stroking her, then moved forward again.

"Oh, God, Mason," she whimpered. It felt so . . . so . . .

He glided deep into her. His pace picked up and his cock stroked her faster. Filling her ass. Again. And again.

She arched her ass upward, wanting him to keep giving her this incredible pleasure.

The simmering embers of her recent orgasm flared to life and joy wafted through her. Building. She moaned as he drove deep, then drew back again.

"I—"

He drove deeper this time and she gasped, pleasure rippling across every nerve ending.

"Mason, you're making me . . . oh, God, yes," she cried at another deep thrust. She trembled at the exquisite sensation. "Making me . . ." Then she moaned, unable to utter another word. Joy pulsed through her and she shuddered, his big cock continuing to fill her, then she wailed at the cataclysmic bliss that jolted through her, expanding to fill her whole being.

She sobbed as he kept thrusting, riding the wave of ecstasy with wild abandon.

Then he drove deep, and held her tight to him. His cock pulsed inside her and she moaned at his guttural groan, and then heat filled her ass.

She trembled in the darkness, blind with the cloth still covering her eyes. The only sound around her the deep ragged breath. Her. Mason. And James.

Finally, Mason drew his cock from inside her and sat on the bench, then drew her toward him. She rested against his solid body.

James shifted and moved away from her. A moment later, she heard a door open and close again.

She and Mason were alone. She could feel it.

Mason's fingers played along the back of her head and the blindfold released. He drew it away. She blinked in the soft light of the room. Mason lifted her to her feet and turned her around, then dragged her into his arms and kissed her with passion. Her arms slid around him as she held him as close as she could.

"You liked that," he murmured against her ear.

"Oh, yes."

His hand glided down her back to her ass and he squeezed her cheek tightly, then smacked it sharply.

"I should punish you for tempting me into letting another man fuck you."

She tipped her head up and as her gaze locked with his, she realized she wanted him to.

"Yes, sir. Punish me."

He groaned.

He dragged her to a nearby table and pushed her torso down on it until her breasts were crushed against the cold, stainless steel surface. His hand smacked against her ass.

"Oh, yes, sir. Harder, please."

He smacked again. Hard this time. Her ass tingled.

"Yes, please, more."

"Fuck, baby." His hand slapped against her tingling flesh again, and she moaned.

He kept slapping her and the pleasure-pain was incredible. She wanted this. And so much more.

He slapped a little lower, near her intimate flesh.

"Oh, yes."

He slapped again and his fingers brushed her folds as he drew his hand back.

He spanked her with short, fast strokes and she arched against him, delighting in the joyous mélange of pleasure and pain. Then to her complete surprise, she moaned as an orgasm jolted through her.

His continuing smacks fueled the fire and she wailed her release.

Finally, his hand came to a halt.

"You might not be able to sit for a week," he observed, dragging his fingertips lightly over her hot, smarting ass.

"But it was so worth it." She smiled. "Sir."

Mason carried Dana down the hall to his bedroom, then set her on her feet. He hadn't been kidding. Her ass was bright red and must sting like hell.

He pulled back the covers and lay down.

"You probably won't want to lie on your back."

She smiled and climbed into the bed, then lay on her

stomach, half on top of him, her arm draped around his waist. He curled his arm around her.

"I'm sure you're right."

One soft breast was crushed against him and her head rested against his chest. He breathed in the lilac scent of her soft, dark hair. He stroked the long strands back from her face and brushed his lips against her forehead.

"Mmm." She sighed contentedly.

God, she had been incredible. He might have suggested she be with James, but everything that had happened after that she had embraced wholeheartedly.

He had been trying to push her away, believing she could never accept his sexual lifestyle, but she had completely surprised him.

She had awakened something in him. With his other subs, everything was predictable. He knew what they wanted and he gave it to them. They satisfied him, too, but there was no real excitement for him.

With Dana, he wanted to explore new things. To find out what excited her. What she wanted and needed. And he had a feeling she would arouse him in ways he had never before anticipated.

His heart thumped in his chest and he cursed himself. This was not supposed to be happening. He was supposed to drive her away.

She sighed against him, her breath washing over his heated skin. Her even breathing told him she was asleep.

She was so sweet. His innocent Dana.

But no more. Now he'd discovered she was a vixen in bed. And adventurous beyond his wildest dreams.

Fuck, what the hell was he going to do now?

Dana woke up snuggled close to Mason, his strong arms around her. Sunlight warmed her cheek. Her eyelids opened and she found Mason's dark blue eyes staring back at her.

"Good morning," he said, his voice husky.

"Good morning." She snuggled closer, and his arms tightened around her.

It was heaven waking up in his arms. Being cradled close to his body. She wanted every day to begin and end like this. Happiness welled through her until she felt she would burst.

"I love you, Mason."

As soon as the words left her mouth, she knew she'd made a mistake. His body stiffened.

It was too much, too soon. They had been making progress. She could feel it. But had those words broken everything?

Mason pushed himself from the bed and walked from the room, not looking back.

Damn it, she'd said she loved him and as much as he loved hearing it, he couldn't encourage her. Of course, he'd been a fucking idiot last night when he'd encouraged her to be with James rather than play on her nervousness and convince her to stop this once and for all. But he couldn't help himself. Once she'd agreed to try being with another man, it was all he could think about. Watching while James stroked her. While he gave her pleasure.

While he made her come.

And it had been exhilarating.

But he'd blown the chance to drive her away. And now . . . she'd said she loved him.

Fuck, his heart said that they could make it work. That Dana had already proven that she could take whatever he gave her, and more.

And that what she wanted excited him. They could find a balance. A shared pleasure that would be deeply arousing for both of them. And satisfying.

But even if that were true, he couldn't expose her to the hell his father would put them through. Mason wanted to protect her, and to do that, he needed to get her away from himself, and far away from his son-of-a-bitch father.

Dana stared at the closed door. Oh, God, she had screwed things up.

She pushed herself from the bed, ready to chase after him, but when she felt the cold, brass doorknob in her hand, instead of turning it, she stopped and rested her head against the door.

What was she doing? Chasing after him was crazy. He'd left because he wanted to get away from her. He needed his space. If he wanted to talk to her, he knew where she was. Going after him would only make things worse.

She sighed and pushed herself from the door, then went into the bathroom. After she'd showered and dressed, she walked out of the room and went to the kitchen. Mason was nowhere to be seen. She even went to the Dark Room and peered inside, in hopes he might be waiting for her there.

But he wasn't.

She made herself some breakfast, sat down in the sunny dining room, and stared out over the city. It wasn't fair. If she had only another day or two with Mason, she didn't want to spend it sitting here on her own.

After she finished eating, she grabbed her cell phone and checked her texts and e-mail, hoping Mason had sent her a message. No luck.

But there was an e-mail from Elli.

WTF, Dana? Are you really sleeping with your brother?

Dana frowned and clicked on the link included in the e-mail.

Her jaw dropped as she stared at the article. It was a tabloid with an awful picture of her and Mason. Out of focus and unflattering, it looked like it had been taken when she was about seventeen. She recognized it as the time she'd tried Rollerblading and had taken a fall. Mason had helped her up, but the angle and the way they'd cropped it made it look like he was pulling her into his arms.

The headline read: MEDIA MOGUL SCREWING HIS SISTER.

Oh, God. The article outright claimed that she and Mason were having sex—which of course she couldn't deny—but it also insinuated that it had been going on ever since she was sixteen. And the reporter made it sound like she was his actual sister.

Oh, God, oh, God, oh, God!

Did Mason know about this?

If he didn't, when he found out, he would freak out.

She slumped in the chair. And he would definitely send her away.

She bit her lip. How much would this affect Mason? Would his business be in trouble? Would he recover?

Her phone vibrated and she picked it up. A text from Mason.

Are you there?

Yes, she tapped into her phone.

The driver will be there in fifteen minutes.

Where am I going? she asked, worried that he would tell her to pack her bags so he could send her away.

No questions. Take off your clothes and wear only your coat and shoes.

She frowned. It didn't sound like he was sending her away. *I only have a jacket with me.*

Then the driver will bring you a coat. Strip now and wear a robe until he arrives.

Yes, sir, she responded.

Twenty minutes later, the doors of the private elevator in the foyer opened and the driver, in his dark suit, stepped into the penthouse. She walked toward him, her hands tightening the ties of the robe around her waist.

"This is for you," he said, holding out a black coat. "And these."

He handed her a bag and she peered inside to see high-heeled, red leather shoes.

It wasn't the usual driver, but Mason probably had more than one.

"Thank you," she said, taking the coat and bag from him.

She walked down the hall to her bedroom and shed the robe, then pulled on the coat. She stepped into the high heels Mason had sent, then walked to the foyer again.

She followed the driver into the elevator, then to the car parked outside the building. He opened the door and she climbed into the backseat, extremely aware of her nakedness under the coat.

Did the driver know?

He climbed into the driver's seat. She pressed her knees together tightly as he turned around.

"He told me to put these on you."

He held up a pair of red handcuffs. Not soft, fluffy cuffs, but solid metal, like real police cuffs, but in some designer red steel.

He opened the cuffs and waited expectantly. Obediently, she held one wrist out and allowed him to snap the cuff around it, then the other. The bite of the cold steel sent a shiver through her.

She sat back in the seat as the car glided forward, wondering where he was taking her.

Since this was the last day of her trial, Mason was probably going to put her through some final trial to drive her away. He wanted her to call it quits, but she wouldn't. No matter what he did to try and scare her away.

If he wanted to be rid of her, he'd have to send her away himself.

The car soon turned onto the highway and sped away from the city. A good half hour passed, then another twenty minutes. Where were they going?

After an hour, the car pulled off the road to a big gate. The gate opened, allowing the car to pass through, then they followed a long, winding driveway to a big house. She'd never seen it before, but Mason was wealthy enough to have several houses.

The driver opened her door and offered his hand. She would have liked to have one hand free to ensure her coat didn't flash open, but with her wrists bound together by the handcuffs, he took both her hands to help her from the car and steady her as she walked.

He accompanied her to the door, then unlocked it and waited for her to enter, then followed her inside.

"Follow me," he said.

She followed the driver down a long hallway, then through a door. This was a different version of the Dark Room. It felt more ominous somehow. The walls were dark-gray brick, the ceiling black. There were chains on

one wall and a big cupboard that probably housed his devices. And very little furniture in the room. Just one large
chair—like a throne—located near the center of the room.

The driver led her toward the chair, but stopped
several feet away, basically in the center of the room. He
pressed a button on a remote control and the clanking of
a heavy chain startled her as it dropped in front of her. Before she realized what was happening, the driver clipped
the chain to her handcuffs, then used the remote to re-
tract the chain, pulling her hands above her head. It kept
going until it became uncomfortable, stretching her arms
upward, pulling her almost to her toes.

"Oh, can you lower it a little, please?" she asked, her
shoulders already starting to ache.

But he ignored her as he set the remote control on the
arm of the big chair, then walked out of the room, closing
the door behind him.

She turned a little, staring at the door, aghast. Then
she lost her balance on the precariously high heels and her
foot tipped over. The shoe fell to the side and slipped away,
so she was forced to stand on her toes.

After a few moments, the uncomfortable position with
one shoe on and one off became intolerable, so she kicked
the other one off, too, and stood on her tippy-toes.

This wasn't like Mason to leave her alone and in discomfort.

She bit her lip. Except when he'd bound her to the
chair.

What challenge was he going to put her through now? Whatever it was, she would prove to him she could handle it.

But the bite of the metal against her wrists, now chafing painfully as she found it harder to hold her body high enough, made her question how long she could hold out.

She heard the doorknob turn and her gaze jerked to the door.

Finally, Mason was here.

But to her complete shock, the man in the doorway was not Mason. It was her stepfather.

"What are you doing here?" she asked.

"Shut up, girl." His nasty, flat-gray eyes focused on her as he walked toward her.

Her skin crawled as his gaze dragged up and down her body. Did he know she was naked under the coat?

She had always been uncomfortable around him, as if he wanted something from her he shouldn't want. But luckily she'd never found herself alone with him before.

He stepped in front of her and she cringed. Then he smiled and, to her horror, ripped the zipper of her coat down and pulled it open.

She gasped, mortified. He pulled a pair of scissors from his jacket pocket, then he cut away the bulk of the garment, leaving only the sleeves and the upper part of the back. Now she stood here, totally exposed to him.

Oh, God, this can't be happening.

He leered at her, staring at her heaving breasts. Finally, he dragged his gaze to her face.

"I'm sure you probably think your brother, Mason, is going to come and find you here, then spirit you away to safety."

She couldn't hide that truth from her eyes and he laughed at the sight. An evil, disturbing laugh.

"You might as well get that thought out of your head right now." He pulled a paper from his pocket and unfolded it, then held it in front of her face. "Mason sold me your contract."

The paper was the recent contract she had signed with Mason with a note scrawled on the bottom in Mason's handwriting stating that he was transferring the contract to his father.

"But he wouldn't do that."

"Are you calling me a liar, girl?" He snatched the paper away and shoved it back in his pocket.

She locked gazes with him, but couldn't hold it. Her memories of cowering from him as a teenager were too raw in her mind. Her stomach was tied up in knots and her cheeks blazed with heat at this intensely disturbing situation.

"Why would he do such a thing?" she finally uttered hoarsely.

He laughed. "Mason has unusual tastes. He is perverted in his sexual interests. He likes to push the limits into forbidden territory." His sharp gaze locked on hers, holding her mesmerized. "He liked the illicitness of fucking his sister."

"Stepsister," she corrected.

He just shrugged. "Did you know he also fucked his step*mother*?"

Her eyes widened. "No. He wouldn't have."

He just laughed again. "You are a stupid little cunt, aren't you." His gaze dropped to her breasts and her breath caught at the blatant lust in his eyes. "But I don't give a fuck how stupid you are. I've been longing to fuck you since I first laid eyes on you." He grinned, making her blood run cold. "Now I finally get the chance."

She gasped as his hand covered her breast and squeezed.

Oh, God, no. This couldn't be happening.

She heard the sound of the door opening and banging against the doorstop. She jerked her head around, desperately hoping it was Mason. That her stepfather was lying and Mason was here to save her.

But Maria stood in the doorway.

Her stepfather scowled. "What the hell are you doing here?" he demanded.

"I can be anywhere the hell I want," Maria answered as she walked into the room, staring at Dana with seeming disinterest. "So you finally got the brat naked and helpless. Well, enjoy the view while you can, because that's all you're going to get."

He scowled. "How did you know I was here?"

"You are a stupid fool. The staff are far more loyal to me than to you. When you gave the driver instructions to bring her here, he texted me to let me know."

Sparks flared in his eyes. "I'll fire that fucking—"

"That's all right. I'll be promoting him to a better position. But right now, I'd say you have other things to worry about. Like what Mason's going to do to you once he finds out what you've done."

Dana started at the sound of a door crashing open and loud footsteps on the hardwood floor of the hall.

"Ah, that sounds like him now."

Mason's frame filled the doorway, and at his first sight of Dana suspended by the chain, naked, he bolted into the room, straight for his father. His fist connected with the man's face, knocking him to the ground. His father growled and pushed himself to his feet, but Mason knocked him down again.

"You fucking stay right there, or I'll make it so you can never stand again."

Dana had never heard Mason so angry before.

"I told you that I'd kill you if you ever touched Dana," he said as he pulled off his coat.

Dana felt the chain lowering and realized Maria had grabbed the remote. As Dana's feet rested on the floor, taking more of her weight, she felt wobbly. Mason threw his coat around her, then scooped her into his arms.

He glared at his father. "I'd like to follow through on that promise right now, but I have more important things to attend to."

He carried Dana from the room. As soon as they were in the hallway, Dana saw two policemen waiting there. Mason nodded and they strode into the room where Maria and Mason's father were waiting.

"I'm so sorry that happened, Dana," he said as he carried her to the front door.

A limo was waiting outside and the driver—the one who usually drove Mason—opened the door. Mason set her on the leather seat inside, then got in beside her.

He put his arm around her and she leaned against his comforting body. Then she began to tremble.

He held her tighter, pressing his lips to the top of her head. "It's okay, baby. You're safe now."

"He told me you sold my contract to him." Her voice came out small and hoarse.

"I would never do that."

"He said . . ." She gazed up at him. "He said you only wanted to be with me because you liked forbidden, illicit sex. He said"—her lip trembled—"that you had sex with my mother."

He frowned. "That's a lie."

Relief washed through her, but she bit her lip. "He actually said your stepmother."

"He means Maria. I had sex with her—you know that—but not since she married my father."

"Oh." She clung to him, glad it was over.

He stroked her back as he continued holding her in the comfort of his arms.

"You don't have to worry about my father hurting you

again," he murmured. "He's going to be up on kidnapping charges, and my private investigator discovered that quite a few of his business practices are questionable. And he hacked into my computer, and my phone. He'll probably be put away for quite a while."

When they finally got home, he gave her a drink and drew her a nice, hot bath. The warmth of the liquor settled into her and calmed her. When she stripped away his coat and climbed into the warm, sudsy water, she insisted he join her. He sat behind her and just held her close.

After the bath, they sat together on the couch in the living room.

"So what now?" she asked.

"As I said, my father will wind up in prison for a very long time. I've also bought up controlling interest in his company." His jaw clenched. "I had promised my mother before she died that I'd do my best to help him stay on his feet, and I wouldn't do anything to show that we had been anything but a happy family. Family had always been so important to her. But my father . . ." Mason scowled. "He always made that difficult. When he leaked our relationship to the press, however, and in the worst possible light, he made that promise I'd made to Mom impossible to keep."

"He did that? My God."

"I've put the shares in Maria's name, so she'll run his company now. She's actually a very savvy businesswoman. She'll ensure everything runs smoothly, and she'll have an allowance allocated to him when he's out of prison, so at least I can keep that part of my promise to my mother."

"You gave the company to Maria?"

He shrugged. "I don't want it."

Dana nodded her understanding, but she couldn't help thinking that he must still have feelings for Maria to have done such a thing.

And now that his father was out of the way . . . maybe he wanted to be with Maria.

"I really meant, what happens with us?"

He gazed down at her. "That's a good question. I know you'll need a little time to recover from all this, but I really think you should go to Paris as soon as possible. I don't want you exposed to the scandal that will continue with the arrest of my father. You don't need to be in the public eye like that. I'll make sure no one knows you're in Paris so you won't be disturbed by the media."

"So you're sending me away?"

He pursed his lips. "Dana, I really think this is for the best."

She nodded, her heart sinking. But she stroked his cheek, longing for the closeness she so desperately needed.

"Please, make love to me, Mason."

"Oh, God, Dana."

He slid his arm under her legs and lifted her up, then carried her to the bedroom. That night he made tender, passionate love to her, making her heart break at the sweetness of it.

．　　　．　　　．

Dana sat on her balcony overlooking the Champs-Élysées. A warm breeze caressed her cheek and she took in the beautiful view, her heart aching.

It had been two weeks since Mason had put her aboard his private jet and sent her away.

It was incredibly beautiful here. It was everything she'd ever dreamed of.

But she would give it up in a heartbeat to be with Mason.

He had sent her away to protect her . . . but also because he didn't want her. He'd tried to be kind. He'd let her know right from the beginning that it would never work between them. When she'd insisted they *could* make it work—that she could be what he needed—he had done his best to prove why that was impossible.

She knew he cared about her, but he didn't *love* her. If he did, then he would have found a way to make it work.

She sighed and stood up, then went back into the apartment. It was luxurious, with an eclectic mix of furniture she loved. Mason had arranged the best for her new life here.

If only he could be a part of it.

Someone knocked on her door and she frowned. She hadn't made any friends here yet. It must be the superintendent coming to check on the faucet handle that kept sticking in the bathroom. She crossed the room and opened the door.

Her heart stopped at the sight of Mason standing in her doorway, a huge bouquet of red roses in his hand.

"Mason?"

He stepped toward her and tugged her into his arms, the flowers dropping to the floor and his mouth claiming hers with passionate intensity.

Her arms glided around his neck and she melted into the kiss.

He pressed her into the apartment and pushed the door closed behind him with his foot. His mouth lifted and she sucked in a breath before he took her mouth again.

"Oh, God, I'll never get enough of this," he said. He held her close, the warmth and hardness of his muscular body sending heat through her.

"You're here," she murmured breathlessly.

"I tried to stay away. Fuck, it nearly killed me, but God help me, I tried."

The joy that had been building in her plummeted at his words. Confusion swirled through her. He was here, but he didn't want to be. She eased away, but he tightened his arms around her, not letting her escape.

"The flowers," she said, glancing at the bundle of roses lying on the floor.

"Leave them."

"But they look so lost and abandoned." She returned her gaze to his, all the pain of his abandonment showing in her eyes. "Cast away."

He rested his hand on her cheek. "I didn't cast you away, Dana. I was only doing what I thought was best."

"So what does this mean, Mason? Where do we go from here?"

"All I knew when I got on the plane was that I couldn't be without you a moment longer." His blue eyes were filled with determination. "I want to find a way to make this work."

Hope welled in her again. She took his hand and drew him further into the room.

"Okay, let's work this out together. You need to control a woman. But you seem most concerned with giving your subs what they want. Maybe it's time to figure out what you want."

"Besides you?"

She smiled. "With me."

"I'll do anything to make you happy."

She rested her hand on his cheek. "It's got to make you happy, too." She smiled. "But I think that what I enjoy will be what you enjoy, too."

She tugged him with her as she backed up to the wall. When she lifted his hand over her head and slid her wrists under his fingers, he took her hint and restrained her.

"Because I like being dominated by you. And being punished by you."

He smiled. "I could tell. It surprised me how much."

"That's because I was with you. Now we have all the

time in the world to find out what gives us pleasure together."

She arched her hips against him, pleased at the feel of his swollen cock.

"Mason, I know you and I will work. Because we love each other."

His lips captured hers in a fierce kiss. "You're right. I do love you. With all my heart. And I never want to let you go."

Joy burst through her at his admission. He loved her.

She arched against him again. "Show me how much. Take me."

He pressed her to the wall, his cock hard and hot against her belly.

His lips brushed against her ear, his breath grazing her neck. "I have a better idea."

Then he released her wrists and stepped back.

"Really? I thought that was a pretty good idea, actually."

He laughed. "In the spirit of us finding our bliss together, why don't you take control?" He turned and walked toward the bedroom, not waiting for her response. "Join me in five minutes."

She stared after him. For a man who'd just suggested she take control, he wasn't exactly letting go of it himself.

She waited impatiently for her watch to tick off the minutes. After exactly five, she hurried to her bedroom door, then pushed it open.

Her breath caught at the sight of Mason, totally naked, kneeling on the floor, his gaze turned downward.

Mason? Being her sub?

Mason sensed her uncertainty. He raised his gaze. "Mistress, what may I do to please you?"

She walked toward him. "I . . . uh . . ." Her gaze glided down his body with a heat that made his blood boil. When her gaze fell on his cock, it began to swell.

"Would you like me to help you undress, Mistress?" he asked.

"Oh . . . no, I . . ." She shook her head, then pulled her top over her head and dropped it. Next, she unfastened her shorts and let them fall to her ankles.

Desire blazed through him at the sight of her breasts swelling from her baby-blue lace bra. He watched with hunger as she reached behind her and unhooked it, then slowly, and purposefully, drew it from her body. Then dropped it to the floor.

He drew in a steadying breath at the sight of her lovely, round breasts. Her nipples tightened under his gaze.

She stepped toward him, until her blue panties were only a breath away.

"You can help me with these," she said.

He tucked his fingers under the elastic and drew them down. Ever so slowly. His pulse increasing as he exposed her intimate parts. He glided the panties down her legs, his gaze locked on her naked pussy. So close he could tip his head slightly and touch it with his tongue.

Which he was sure he'd be doing seconds from now.

She stepped backward, out of her panties. Then moved close again. She rested her hands on his shoulders and stroked. He could feel the love in her touch. God, he'd missed her so much.

"I want you to . . . uh . . ." She gazed down at him. "Please lick my pussy."

She didn't have to say please, but he wasn't about to correct her. He leaned forward and brushed his tongue over her folds. Then he leaned back again.

"Oh, I want you to do it again."

Her uncertainty was utterly charming. He leaned in and licked her again, this time teasing at the folds a little. She widened her stance, giving him better access, but he moved away again, awaiting her next instruction.

"I don't know how this works. I want you to . . . you know . . . make me come."

"Just tell me what you want and I'll follow your instructions."

"But you do it perfectly without instructions," she pouted.

He chuckled. "Thank you, Mistress."

She frowned and thought for a moment, then she smiled. "I know. You will follow any command, right?"

"Yes, Mistress."

"Good, then I command you to take control."

He tipped his head as he gazed up at her. "You don't even want to give this a try?"

She shrugged. "I don't need to. You've shown me enough for me to know what I like." She smiled. "And I like you in control."

"And if I refuse, will you punish me?"

Dana laughed, but the thought of slapping her hand across his rock-hard ass made her drip with need.

"How about you don't refuse, but then order me to punish you?"

He stood up and walked to her bed, then bent over it, his ass in the air. "Show me the goods first."

She walked toward him, her insides quivering. She lifted her hand, then smacked across his flesh, a little timidly. The feel of his hard flesh and the stinging of her hand were invigorating. She slapped his ass again and heat swelled through her body.

She slapped twice more, harder. His skin turned a pinkish red. After two more slaps, he growled, then suddenly she felt herself tumbling onto the bed, with him prowling over her. His big, naked body covered hers, his cock swollen and hot against her stomach.

"You like punishing me." His eyes glowed with heat.

She grinned. "I could get into it. Maybe it would be better if I handcuffed you next time."

He grabbed her wrists and pushed them over her head. "Maybe it would be better if I overpowered and fucked you instead."

She arched against him, her desire for him blossoming into a desperate need. "I think that's a great idea," she said hoarsely.

He pressed his pelvis hard against her, his thick cock grinding into her belly. "You seem to have forgotten how to address me."

"Oh. I think that's a great idea, *sir*."

"Now tell me what you want."

"I want you to fuck me, sir."

His midnight eyes darkened to almost black. He pressed his cock to her slickness and stroked, then pushed into her. His wide cockhead separated her, then moved forward. Slowly. As he filled her with his thick shaft.

She dropped her head back. "Oh, God, that feels so good."

He pushed forward a little faster, until his full length was immersed in her.

She squeezed him and he moaned.

"God, I've missed you," he said, his eyes blazing with need.

"Show me, sir. Fuck me until I scream."

He growled, then drew back and thrust deep into her, making her gasp. He began to pump, filling her again and again with his solid shaft. She whimpered softly, loving the feel of him inside her. Thrusting into her.

She arched against his restraining hand, but he held on tight. Pleasure swelled higher with each stroke.

"I love you so much, sir."

He began to thrust faster, driving deeper. She moaned, squeezing him inside her.

"Call me Mason. When you come . . . say my name."

She smiled, then sucked in a breath as her senses spun and her insides quivered. "Yes, Mason."

The pleasure rose higher and higher.

"I'm so close. Oh, Mason, you're going to make me . . ."

He groaned as she squeezed him.

Blissful sensations quivered through her and she moaned. "Yes. Oh, I'm . . ." She sucked in a breath. "Oh, Mason," she wailed, plummeting over the edge.

He groaned and at the feel of his hot liquid release, she gasped, then shattered in ecstasy.

Mason held her close, the two of them gasping for breath. His cock was still embedded inside her and he had never felt so complete.

How had he ever believed he could let her go? She was everything to him.

And he would spend every day of the rest of his life proving to her just how much he loved her.